Toil Under the Sun

Toil Under the Sun

Book One

The Leighton Family Saga

Vicki Hopkins

Dedication

To Phoebe Holland, née Edwards, my third great-grandmother, who chose to end her life November 13, 1862, in the metropolitan borough of Bolton, Greater Manchester, England. She hanged herself while in a state of unsound mind.

Table of Contents

Chapter One 9
    Toil Under the Sun
Chapter Two 19
    Blood Isn't Always Thicker
Chapter Three 29
    The Serpent
Chapter Four..36
    Violence Settles Nothing
Chapter Five..46
    An Unsound Mind
Chapter Six 54
    The Ways of Women
Chapter Seven 63
    More Harm Than Good
Chapter Eight..75
    Taking Care of Our Own
Chapter Nine..82
    Luck or Fate?
Chapter Ten..90
    Tea for Two
Chapter Eleven 98
    Brains or Brawn
Chapter Twelve 108
    The Aftermath of Terror
Chapter Thirteen 115
    The Art of Courting

Chapter Fourteen 125
    The Sibling Gap
Chapter Fifteen... 133
    Every Flower Has a Meaning
Chapter Sixteen 141
    The Calling Card
Chapter Seventeen.. 150
    The Battle Field
Chapter Eighteen 158
    The Blessing
Chapter Nineteen.. 167
    Graveyard of Bitterness
Chapter Twenty... 175
    The Greatest of Gifts
Chapter Twenty-One... 183
    Sensational Outrage
Chapter Twenty-Two... 191
    Consequences
Chapter Twenty-Three... 201
    The Visit
Chapter Twenty-Four 209
    A New Beginning
Chapter Twenty-Five 217
    An Untimely End
Chapter Twenty-Six... 224
    The Prodigal
Chapter Twenty-Seven... 233
    A Partnership Begins
Epilogue 241

About The Leighton Family Saga............................. 245

About the Author.. 246

Chapter One

Toil Under the Sun

Manchester, July 1866

A bead of sweat trickled down William's forehead, rolled over his brow, and dropped into his right eye. The salty liquid stung, and with an annoyed sweep of the back of his dirty hand, he wiped away the perspiration.

He couldn't remember a summer so hot in the twenty-five years of his life. Every laborer in Manchester complained about the stifling heat, from the cotton mills to the brickyards. This particular weather event had been brutal in a city filled with smokestacks that spewed out the filth of factories. The sky, rather than being blue, turned into a hazy brown that hung lifeless overhead. With no breeze to bring an ounce of relief, it was a wonder that the sun penetrated through the thick of it, further torturing the workers who toiled underneath.

"Come on, lads; put your back into it. We're behind schedule." Thorpe, the foreman on the job, shouted his displeasure.

The crew kept silent with their heads lowered and eyes focused on the task. Brick upon brick they erected the walls of a new warehouse on Church Street that would climb four stories in height. At present, it stood five feet around the parameter, as they had barely been on the job a week. Construction would be long and backbreaking as scaffolding climbed upward, aiming for the rooftop.

William slapped a layer of mortar on the row of bricks with his trowel and smoothed it across the top. "Slave to none," he mumbled under his breath. The phrase had been one that rolled about in his mind like a mantra from the faraway land of India, keeping his goals before him. One day he would be the master and not the laborer sweating like a hog in the hot afternoon sun.

His father and grandfather had lived the trade, and William grew into manhood knowing no other skill. Though his ancestors worked for generations laying bricks, the family had nothing lasting to show for their work. Instead, William, like his parents before him, lived in a tiny row house on Swan Road. The horrific slums of Angel Meadows lay blocks away from his door, and its stench, hopelessness, and poverty reminded him daily of his low class in the scheme of English society.

As far as siblings, his two brothers fared no better in life. The only difference between the three boys had been that William learned to read and write. A small window of opportunity for an education opened at their local church when he turned six. After a few years of schooling, his father pulled him out and sent William to the brickfields like his older brothers had worked before him. Eager to better himself, he continued to learn through reading books whenever the opportunity arose.

By the time he left school, his speech differed

from the rest of the family too. His strict instructor had no qualms about striking him with a rattan cane on the palm of his hand each time William said "me" instead of "my" or used the local slang. The man's dreadful, grating voice still rang in his ears, reminding him of the painful punishment.

"You best learn to talk the Queen's English," he ranted, slapping him repeatedly until welts formed like snakes slithering across his skin. "You'll never get anywhere in this life, boy, if you do not talk like an educated lad."

Eventually he realized that his ability to read and write when his other family members could not had been a blessing and a curse. Because he could sign his name in perfect penmanship, it elicited jealousy from his brother Hugh, who merely marked his signature with a scribbled *X*.

William positioned a brick on the mortar and used the handle of the trowel to tap it in place, lessening the air bubbles underneath the block. With the sharp edge of the tool, he scraped off the excess mortar. The hod carrier hobbled toward the workers with another load. William had carried thousands of bricks on his shoulders since he was a young boy and had laid a thousand more when he was old enough to learn the craft.

Another bead of sweat rolled down his forehead, and he rubbed it away before it stung his eyes. He glanced at the empty water pail from a day's worth of workers gulping the liquid to quench their thirst. The foreman hadn't noticed it lay dry or didn't care.

"Hey, Teddy," William shouted at one of the young boys on the crew. "See that bucket over there?

Go fill it up."

The lad glanced up at Thorpe for permission, who shot William an irritated squint for giving orders.

"Make it quick, and no fooling around," he barked.

"Aye, boss," Teddy answered, grabbing the bucket and running off to the spigot of the nearest public fountain.

William adjusted his cap, wishing it had a wider rim to protect his face from the sun. He chuckled, thinking one of his mother's hats might do a better job. They had another two hours of labor before quitting time.

"These bricks are shite." Bailey, a coworker, grumbled after tapping one in place. "What company made these?"

"Don't know," William replied in a low tone, not wanting the foreman to catch their conversation. "I agree though. Not the best quality." He glanced at other buildings nearby. "Give it a few years and they'll be covered with black soot anyway from the factories. No one will notice whether they be good or bad."

"Don't look like Manchester union men made this lot. You think the contractor got them from outside the district to save a few quid?"

"Perhaps a carter snuck the lot in from Stockport," William suggested. His brow crinkled at the idea of using bricks from outside the Manchester city line. If it was true, it meant more trouble.

"You going to the union meeting next week?" Bailey inquired. He stood erect, stretched his back, and groaned. Afterward, he removed his hat, wiped the sweat from his brow, and put it back.

"Yeah, I'll be there with Hugh."

"I'll mention the matter to the union delegates," Bailey said, "and see if one of 'em can look into it. If they're from Stockport, some bloke will pay for his cheating."

"As long as nobody gets hurt," William harshly replied, narrowing his eyes. "I dislike the union violence. Makes no sense to hurt people and their family members over a damn brick." He slopped a lump of mortar on top of the row in irritation, and it splattered on his shirt.

"Bloody hell, Leighton, if we don't look out for ourselves, nobody else will," Bailey said in a throaty growl. "We either protect our livelihood or starve."

"Fine, but don't ask me to come and hamstring a horse or throw lighted naphtha through some master brickmaker's window. I'll have no part of it." His voice snapped in return. The loathing emotions he held about the violent union acts sickened his stomach.

Bailey narrowed his eyes and pondered a moment. "How 'bout I suggest a few lads come here at midnight and knock down our fine work. Then the contractor will have to buy new bricks from a reputable source inside the district lines." Bailey glanced at Thorpe to make sure he wasn't listening. "They'll have to call us back, so at least we'll get a few more shillings of pay."

The thought of their labor destroyed by a bunch of union hooligans angered William. He had poured enough sweat into this job to take it personally. Bailey was right about one point. They worked an average of fifty-five hours a week for a pittance of thirty shillings. An extended few weeks of toil would ensure added income. He needed to make as much money as he could during the summer months before Manchester gray skies returned along with rain and cold. The lack of daylight hours would diminish their working time.

William's eye caught sight of the young lad returning with a bucket of water. Both his hands wrapped around the handle as he struggled to hold it steady. The water sloshed over the sides, splashing onto the thirsty, dry ground. If he didn't help the boy, there'd be nothing left to drink.

William left his spot and quickly incurred Thorpe's wrath.

"Where the hell are you going, Leighton?"

Ignoring the interrogation, William pushed past him and sprinted toward the lad. Teddy's face, red and dripping with sweat, looked as if it would burst at any minute from the weight of the haul.

"Here, let me help you with that, boy," he declared, grabbing the handle to relieve his struggles.

"Thanks," he gasped. "I done thought I'd drop it for sure. Mr. Thorpe would smack me good."

"Happy to help," William replied, carrying the water back to the work site.

When they arrived, William put the bucket down in a small spot of shade. He grabbed the ladle, dipped it into the water, and offered the boy a drink.

"Here you go. You deserve it after all that effort."

Teddy took it to his lips. He gulped a good portion and then wiped his mouth with his sleeve. William slurped the remaining water and then handed the spoon back. "Now, why don't you give everybody here a drink before they pass out from the heat? Can you do that for me?"

Thorpe neared them. "Enough, Leighton. Get

back to work."

Rather than wasting his breath arguing, he returned and grabbed another brick. Thorpe dipped the ladle into the bucket and took a hearty drink. Angered by his selfishness, William nearly cursed the man aloud but refrained.

Thorpe gave the empty dipper to the lad. "Go ahead and serve the rest."

"Aye, boss," Teddy replied. He scooped water and headed to Bailey.

"Thanks, lad." After taking a drink, he handed the ladle to Teddy. There were three hod carriers for the six bricklayers on the job. The bucket would soon be empty.

As the day wore on and their work neared completion, William wondered how his older brother faired in his new adventure. Twenty years his senior, Aaron had left the household when William was a baby. The vast age difference prevented any close relationship between them as siblings, but recently Aaron had been on William's mind.

His elder brother remained in Leyland, where they grew up. Aaron had an unfortunate turn of luck financially and decided to emigrate to Australia. Enticed by the promise of work to build houses for the influx of settlers in Victoria, he couldn't resist the opportunities that supposedly awaited. With his wife and eight children, he boarded a ship from Liverpool that would reach their destination over three and a half months later. William waited for word of their arrival, worried about their safety on the long voyage.

His departure had left their mother, Martha, severely distraught and inconsolable. The reality of never seeing her firstborn again and her eight grandchildren broke her spirit. William had cared for his elderly mother since the passing of their father seven years earlier. Once a vibrant woman, she had changed into a downcast and lonely soul who often spoke of her discontent of life. In all honesty, William didn't know how to help her, and the burden lay heavily on his shoulders.

The workday slipped into dusk. William and the rest of the crew went their separate ways to their families and homes. It took fifteen minutes to walk to his residence from the work site. Though the temperature had cooled, a pang of worry rose about how his mother coped with the stifling temperatures throughout the day. He dreaded entering their dwelling that heated like a baker's oven.

As he turned the corner and spotted the open door, he saw his mother sitting on the two-step stoop, holding her head in her hands. Her gray hair amassed on top of her head in an unkempt bun that hadn't been washed or combed in weeks. A rip in her old cotton blouse exposed her upper chest. She appeared as if she had aged another year since William departed that morning.

"Mam, what are you doing out here?" He approached and stood before her slumped body and lowered head. Nearby neighbors stood outdoors for relief from the heat, leaning against the soot-covered buildings in which they lived. They watched him as he waited for an answer, but she said nothing.

"Have you had anything to drink?" William lifted her chin with his hand, and her empty eyes looked at him in return. It broke his heart to see the once lively woman broken and old. She shook her head no.

"Let me get you water," he said. He stepped indoors, shocked at the disarray. His mother hadn't cooked dinner or done any chores. After he grabbed a metal cup, he walked across the street to the public fountain and pumped out a refreshing drink. When he returned to her side, his mother remained downcast.

"Here. Take a sip." William offered the cup, bringing it to her lips.

"Don't want," she mumbled. "Just let me die."

"I'm not going to let you die, Mam. You're just thirsty. Now drink," he firmly ordered. She glanced up at him and looked at the cup. Her lips, dry and cracked, parted. William pushed the container against the parched flesh. "Drink," he ordered, sounding as if his father's voice had come out of him from beyond the grave.

Too weak to argue, she took a sip. After tasting the cold liquid, her shaky hands grasped the cup, and she drank the rest on her own.

"Have you eaten today?" She didn't answer. "Come on, Mam. Let's go inside, open the windows, and have something to eat."

William pulled her upright to her wobbly legs. "You'll have to mend that torn blouse," he said. "You're such a good seamstress. Do you need me to buy you some thread?" His mother remained silent as they returned indoors, and he led her to the rocking chair.

Even though he had worked twelve hours laying bricks, the day had not ended. He scanned the turmoil of their home and sighed.

"Slave to none," he whispered, expelling an

exhausted sigh from his lungs. The words failed to encourage as his life remained a never-ending sentence of drudgery.

Chapter Two

Blood Isn't Always Thicker

Hugh Leighton walked a step ahead of Eliza, his wife, who held their eight-month-old daughter, Margaret, in her arms. Early that morning they argued, making it three days in a row they fought like bickering siblings. To be honest, he couldn't remember what their latest fight had been about, thinking now it was a waste of energy.

He had fallen infatuated with Eliza, the sister of one of his union friends, two years ago after their introduction at a pub. Her hair the color of honey and her lips a natural pink tint instantly drew his attention. At first he thought her personality reserved, but after they married, Hugh discovered the woman could be a handful when she got riled up. Eliza didn't fit the picture of a perfect submissive wife that he had hoped for in a mate. Regardless of his slight disappointment, he had a spouse and children. As far as being in love, he wasn't quite sure what those emotions entailed. Marriage, to Hugh, was merely a state of existence that had not been an easy road.

Their firstborn baby, Thomas, died two weeks after birth. Hugh woke up one morning and discovered him dead. He expected to pick up a fine-looking young lad but instead found a cold body with closed eyes and clenched fists. The pride he held as a father evaporated into a grim emotion of resentment and grief. He had never been one for shedding a tear about anything in his life until that day when he held the lifeless form of his firstborn.

Eliza, distraught as he, in due course, became pregnant again not long afterward. Even though over a year had passed since his son's death, the pain gnawed at him in spite of his wife bearing him a daughter. The baby looked healthy enough, but fear clung to Hugh like a deep-seated thorn in his soul that she too would be dead before he saw his grave.

Babies and children died every day in Manchester. The poor expected nothing less in a world where mouths were often void of sustenance and disease lurked around every corner from an outbreak of smallpox, cholera, or diphtheria. Manchester had been coined hell on earth in some areas, crawling with rats, crime, filth, and the stench of sewage. If that wasn't enough, the air choked with chimney smoke that left most residents wheezing and coughing. On hot days, it lay as a layer—brown and unmovable as a thick blanket. The morbid surroundings had become the devil's playground.

Hugh trudged toward Swan Lane, bearing one more burden on his shoulders. William, his younger brother of five years, had begged him to visit because their mother had not been well. His brother had cared for her since the day their father died seven years earlier. William possessed more patience than he did when it came to the ways of the elderly. He and Eliza had moved twice from Blackburn to Bolton and then to Manchester where they lodged a few miles from each other. Apparently, his mother pined over her firstborn who left the country. Hugh thought his mother self-centered because William deserved more affection than he received for his sacrifice to care for her in her old age.

As brothers, William and Hugh were not close and held differing political and religious views. They were often at odds about matters of the union, ending up in shouting matches and name-calling. Hugh had no qualms in fighting for the rights of laborers even if it meant violence. He had joined in a few vicious incidences himself, which included the destruction of property, physical assaults, and bringing a gun. He hadn't shot anyone yet but did kill a guard dog. It was either the hound or him as it bared its sharp teeth and charged at him in the brickyard.

The business owner had employed nonunion men. Similar to other defiant masters who refused to pay their dues and obey the rules, Hugh made sure he got what was coming to him. A group of men destroyed over ten thousand bricks, burned his barn, and killed the dog. It had been a severe price to pay, which the newspapers termed another "outrage" of enforcement. As soon as William learned of the matter, he balked about the use of force, blaming the union that they did no good by harming the masters. Hugh hoped his visit wouldn't turn into another row about union matters because he wasn't in the mood to squabble with his brother's self-righteous attitudes.

"Hugh, wait up," Eliza called. He hadn't realized his ruminating about life had caused him to sprint ahead. He halted, spun around, and saw Eliza a few yards behind him, out of breath, clutching their crying daughter.

"Sorry, love." He reached out and took the baby. "Here, let me take her. We're almost there."

"Thank you," Eliza replied, handing Margaret into his grasp. "You were stomping down the road like you were marching to war."

"I feel like I'm at war," he countered. After cradling Margaret in his arms a few moments, she halted her tears.

"She's hungry," Eliza said. "I'll feed her when we get there."

"Just a couple more blocks to go, little one," Hugh said in a calming tone, touching her button nose with his fingertip. If he needed to, he could soften his voice for any little lady. Margaret gazed at him like a porcelain doll with curly blond hair like her mother's and bright blue eyes. Her cheeks were pink as a rosebud.

They resumed their walk, strolling at a leisurely pace, and arrived a few minutes later. The neighborhood where William settled appeared no better than where they lived. Brick terrace houses as far as the eye could see in long rows, with soaring chimney stacks dotting the landscape above the roofs. The heat wave had subsided to some extent, and the murky air that hung above the city from the factories lessened, thanks to a hearty breeze that had picked up the evening before.

Hugh knocked on the door, and William opened it straightaway. With Margaret in his arms, he amused himself by teasing his brother. "I'm pretty good at holding babies," he proclaimed with a sly grin. "About time you married and had one of your own."

William grimaced as he usually did when Hugh brought up the subject. "I have enough to do besides women and babies," he replied in an irked tone. "Besides, Mam and me we do just fine without crying babies, don't we?" He glanced at his mother, who sat in her rocking chair in the shadows of the room.

Martha lifted her head. "Suppose we do," she responded, attempting to rise to her feet. After a deep moan to stand upright, she shuffled toward Hugh.

He hadn't seen his mother in a few months. The skin on her face looked pale and shallow, and she had lost a considerable amount of weight. Wrinkles etched her face in deep grooves, and puffy bags accented her eyes. She smelled as if she hadn't bathed in weeks, and her hair looked like the nest of a bird.

"Let me hold the little lass," his mother entreated, reaching out to take her from his arms.

"You sure you can hold her tight?" Hugh scowled, concerned about her strength to hold anything besides a cup of tea.

William interjected. "Why don't you sit back down, Mam. Hugh will let you hold the babe in your arms while you're sitting."

"Let me help you." Eliza stepped forward with a worried glint in her eye. She took Martha's arm and led her to the chair.

"Has she been eating?" Hugh leaned in and whispered to William.

"Barely."

"I don't like the look of her."

Eliza situated Martha firmly in the rocker and

then took the baby and assisted Martha as she cradled Margaret in her arms. His mother appeared confused and unsure of herself, but Eliza kept close to her side and one hand on the baby.

"We should talk," William said, grabbing Hugh's arm and leading him out the door for a private conversation.

Hugh glanced over his shoulder, reluctant to leave. Margaret started to wail again in unfamiliar arms.

"She's hungry, Martha, do you mind if I hold and feed her?" Eliza asked. Not waiting for an answer, Eliza pulled Margaret back to her breast, and Hugh sighed that she was safe in strong arms.

"I don't know what to do." William's raspy voice expressed as they reached the outdoors. "I'm gone over twelve hours a day, and she's left here alone by herself. I can't care for her any longer."

Hugh looked at William, anticipating what his brother was about to say next. "Before you even ask, I'm not about to bring her in me home. I'm gone all day too, you know. Eliza is overwhelmed with our daughter and the neighbor's three young offspring she watches while they work at the mill." He peered into the room and considered his mother's frailty. "Isn't there a neighbor or someone who can check in on her when you're gone?"

"Not really," he replied with an exasperated sigh. William frowned, obviously frustrated. "You're putting me in a troublesome spot." His face contorted into a pleading expression.

"Sorry but nothing I can do." Hugh remained adamant.

"I'm at my wit's end, for heaven's sake," he lashed out. "I've taken care of Mam since Papa died, while you and Aaron live your lives as you please with your wives and children. Ever since Aaron left, she acts as if she doesn't want to live any longer."

Without forethought, Hugh gushed forth. "I suppose you wouldn't consider an asylum." Soon after the words left his mouth, he regretted the suggestion. William's nostrils flared, and his eyes grew dark. They were not the typical reaction his docile brother expressed since he always did the right thing. The man's conscience was his worst enemy, but if he wanted to continue to shoulder the burden, he would have to find help elsewhere or put their mother away.

"What about the church? You're always spouting off about that parish of yours and the good folk you worship with on Sunday. Can't you talk to the vicar about getting help from the congregation?"

William shifted irritably in his stance. "What would you know about good folk at church?" he snarled, expressing his irritation.

"Nothing," he truthfully answered. "You know I hate religion. God can sod off as far as I'm concerned."

"You're no help at all," William murmured. He spun around and walked indoors.

Hugh followed him and walked over to his mother, watching Eliza breastfeed the babe.

"Isn't she a sweet one, Mam?" He smiled down at her with pride, but as he did so, a pang of grief stabbed his heart, recalling the face of his son.

His mother didn't reply. She stared at the child in Eliza's arms for another minute, and then a tear trickled down her cheek.

"Had all boys, I did. Would have liked a little girl," her voice quavered. "Don't matter now. You'll all leave me one day like Aaron did. Sailed off to a faraway place with me grandbabies never to be seen again. I'll die alone."

Perhaps he should have regretted Aaron's departure as well but thought his brother somewhat foolhardy to risk everything on a whim halfway around the world. His mother had the right to mourn his loss, as she would never see him again or the children.

Hugh put his arm around her shoulder for comfort and bent down. "William and I aren't going anywhere, Mam. Stop your fussing. You have a fine grandchild here. More to come." He lifted his eyes to Eliza. "Isn't that right, wife?"

Eliza returned a strained smile.

"And look at William here. One of these days he's bound to get married and start giving you more grandbabies." Even though he tried to be positive, his mother would hear none of it.

"I've lived too long," she moaned with tears welling in her eyes. "I miss me husband. Gone too. Dead and buried."

"Now no more talk of dying. You got plenty of years ahead," Hugh interjected in stern speech. "William here takes good care of you, and I'm not far away. Few miles, that's all."

Guilt should have been the emotion Hugh held for not offering to help, but he just didn't have the stomach to take in an old lady into their cramped dwelling. They barely made their rent and had food on the table. William had no wife or child to support, so it just made good sense to leave their elderly mother with him and find somebody to lend a helping hand.

The baby started to wail, and Eliza peered at Hugh with pleading eyes. She wanted to leave, and frankly, he did too. William would consider them rude for running off so soon.

"See you at the union meeting next week?" Hugh asked. He took his hand off his mother's shoulder and stood upright.

"Yes, I'll be there," his brother responded with little enthusiasm.

"Hey, I've heard rumors the warehouse Ashworth has you lads building is using nonunion bricks. That true?"

"Don't know. Right now I don't care either." William twisted away from him again and ran his fingers through his hair in exasperation. Hugh regarded the worrisome frown on his brother's face. There was no use fighting in front of their mother or Eliza and the baby for that matter.

"Come on, wife. Let's be going." Hugh approached and bent down to kiss his mother's cheek. "Now you take care of yourself, Mam. Get some food in your belly. You're looking too skinny—like a twig you are." She didn't reply but lifted her gaze toward him. The look in her dim gray eyes left an uneasy feeling in his gut. For a second she acted as if she wanted to say something but couldn't get the words out. Hugh turned toward William.

"Next week then. We have plenty of union business to discuss."

"Next week," William countered, walking him to

the door.

Eliza held the baby firmly to her chest. She stood in front of his brother and glanced at William sadly.

"Take care." Her kind tone tried to soothe his worry.

"Always have," he answered. "Probably always will. No good relying on others."

Hugh knew by the look in William's eyes that the sour remark was meant for his ears. Honestly, he didn't care. His brother, who always acted smarter than him, could figure it out on his own.

Chapter Three

THE SERPENT

The blackness of the room enveloped Martha as she sat alone in her rocking chair. Her feet pushed herself back and forth, creating the swaying movement she found relaxing. With her eyes closed, she stirred the memories of her life and waited for the ghosts of bygone days to rise from the dead. A sigh of relief expelled from her lips as the rocking stirred a breeze cooling her face. The longer she swayed, the more lifelike her visions emerged. Eventually the muddled imaginations cleared, and there in front of her stood her husband, tall and handsome as the day she met him nearly fifty years earlier.

"What are you doing, Martha?" his smooth voice asked with a twinkle in his eye.

"Just relaxing, love," she answered, keeping her eyes closed.

"You look tired, Martha. I've missed you." His loving tone soothed her anxiety.

In Martha's illusory state of mind, John walked toward her and knelt next to her chair. He put his hand on top of her wrinkled skin and bony fingers, and the sensation of his cold flesh caused her to flinch.

As the moments stretched into quiet minutes, his touch warmed.

When they were young, his roguish ways had attracted her the first time they crossed paths at a town get-together in Leyland. The weavers, of which her father was one, occasionally joined with other locals at the assembly hall. Men and women worked in their homes with their looms, weaving fabrics for the merchants. The solitary trade gave them reason to gather for socializing and dancing.

"Do you remember the night we met?" Martha asked.

"How can I forget?" he answered. "There you were, standing alone by yourself in your blue frock and shawl, looking like a wallflower. You thought you were unnoticed, but I noticed you. You were so pretty with your strawberry blonde hair, rosy cheeks, and a stunning smile."

Martha snickered. "I knew you were a rogue the moment I laid eyes on you, John Leighton. That fancy name of yours, your tall stature, dark hair, and brown eyes. All the girls thought you were a good catch, but I had heard rumors you were a ladies' man."

"A bricklayer a rogue?" John laughed. "Hardly, my dear." Martha opened her eyes to look on his face. To her disappointment, it vanished, and the empty room met her blurry gaze. She continued to rock herself back and forth. After leaning her head back, closing her eyes once more, she floated back into memories.

It didn't take long to fall in love with John and wed. Before she knew it, they had their first child who they named Aaron after John's father.

"Do you remember our boy Aaron?"

"Handsome young babe with a full head of hair when he was born."

John's sweet voice returned, and Martha swore she felt the heat of his breath on her face when he spoke. Not wishing to break the spell, she kept her eyes closed and her hands tightly clutching the arms of the chair as if she held his hand.

"Our firstborn. He was a good baby. Hardly ever cried and grew up to be a fine young man."

"An adventurous lad, as I remember."

"Adventurous indeed," Martha whimpered. "He's left me now for some faraway land—taken his wife and our grandbabies with him." A tear trickled down her cheek. "No thought of the heartbreak it would cause me."

Her husband didn't respond straightaway, and Martha feared he had left her side. A moment later his voice returned. "Don't you remember the Bible, Martha? Isn't a man supposed to leave his father and mother and cling to his wife?"

Still recounting scriptures, Martha thought to herself. She didn't want his rebuke only his sympathy.

"But you died and left me, and I clung to Aaron." Martha defended herself.

"And William clung to you."

She could not argue that William had done so as Aaron and Hugh had married and birthed children of their own. The young man had put aside finding a wife because of her needs. A pang of guilt about her ungratefulness for his sacrifice poked at her old soul.

Martha ceased rocking and got herself to her feet. She opened her eyes and caught the rays of the moonlight streaming through a crack in the torn cotton curtains on the front window. The chair behind her ceased moving, and she shuffled toward the dirty glass to look out at the night sky. William had told her that he would be home late because of a meeting at the union. She let out a lonesome moan and gazed outdoors, peering at the row house across the street. Most people had retired for bed.

"No one but me," she said, shattering the silence in the room. "Just the ghosts of the past."

Her eyes caught sight of a young man walking down the street, and his height and mannerisms reminded her of Sidney, who she had often envisioned as a grown lad. Excited to see him, she ran to the door and flung it open. Screaming from the threshold, she called his name.

"Sidney! Sidney! Where are you going?" Martha stepped outdoors and watched the boy continue to walk away paying her no attention. "Sidney stop!" She stepped on the stoop about to run after him when the fellow turned around at glowered at her.

"Me name isn't Sidney," he shouted. "Get back in the house, you crazy old hag." He stomped onward and turned the corner out of sight.

Martha's brow furrowed as a wave of confusion suddenly cleared. She realized that she stood outdoors in her bare feet, screaming the name of her son who had died at birth. Remorseful about her moment of unstable thoughts, she retreated indoors, closed the door, and sat back down in the rocker. Her body trembled.

"Should have told Hugh and William about Sidney," she said, breaking the silence of the room.

"Why didn't we tell them?" Her husband's voice

returned. "I can't seem to remember."

"Aaron was too young to understand—only just turned two," Martha replied. She thought for a moment as to the reason. "Heartbreak, I guess. No use passing on heartbreak to the children."

"Aye, better not to speak of it," the ghostly voice of John somberly replied.

Martha closed her eyes and resumed rocking back and forth with more fervency than before.

"Hugh and William, they fight all the time, love. Like cats and dogs, they are far different in thoughts and such."

"Sibling rivalry, I surmise," her husband replied with a hint of laughter. "They always fought as youngsters. Don't you remember, Martha? Shoving, punching, pulling each other's hair."

"How can I forget?" She giggled. The scenes of their throwing blows at one another and wrestling on the grass brought a moment of levity to her heart. Nowadays though, as men, they fought about other things.

"Don't care for each other, not one bit," she announced as if John didn't already know. "Politics, religion, all those high and mighty things that divide men. I reckon they will never be close."

John's voice did not return. Instead, she sensed a dark and more sinister presence enter the unlit room. Goose bumps rose upon her arms, and she stiffened. A subtle and menacing voice whispered in her ears.

"Look at you. The boy was right. You're an old hag, alone, crazy, and no one cares." The accusations hissed like a snake.

She could not deny it. Her beauty had faded into

obscurity as if it never existed. At one time her pretty face caused the heads of men to turn. Her figure was perfect, and her complexion flawless. Now her frame was nothing more than that of a shriveled piece of flesh, etched with deep wrinkles, and eyesight as murky as a foggy morning.

Alone—that too was true. She'd spend hours alone while William worked and attended meetings. No friends and no family. Aaron sailed away. She would never see him or his wife and children again.

Crazy—perhaps so. One moment she could remember and the next she could not. Her low spirits had sapped her strength, and the emptiness inside haunted her mind.

But did no one care? Didn't the Bible say the devil was a liar?

"William cares," she murmured. "I may be old and alone, but William cares."

Like the serpent in the garden, the voice returned to tell her otherwise. "But you heard him tell Hugh how much of a burden you are and to take you to his home instead. Your son tires of you."

The weight of the serpent's words bore down on Martha's heart until the breath in her lungs dissipated. When she tried to inhale, it felt as if her airway closed and she was suffocating.

"Cannot breathe?" the voice tempted. "That's how William feels. He's smothering, taking care of an old woman day in and day out. You're nothing but a load on his shoulders like a hod of bricks, killing him slowly when it's you who should die."

"Lie— Liar," Martha gasped. Her hand clutched her neck as she gasped for air to fill her lungs. "Get behind me, devil!" she squawked.

The devil's laughter filled her ears, and Martha called out for her dead husband to return. "John! John!"

Tears streamed down her cheeks as she waited for his loving voice to bring calm to her soul. In its place the sound of her heart pounded in her ears. The atmosphere in the room grew quiet once more as she frantically rocked to and fro in the chair. After a few minutes passed, her mind regained peace. Except for the overwhelming sense of loneliness, she felt nothing else. No fear or remorse. The memories faded, refusing to resurrect.

Control returned, but her body weak and old ached for rest. An overwhelming urge to climb the stairs and go bed pulled her upward from the chair. She lumbered across the wooden planks and placed one foot upon the first step. Fourteen more waited her cold feet. Inhaling a deep breath, she took the second. When her eyes lifted to the landing above, she saw John with his arms outstretched, bidding her to come.

"Time for bed, Martha," he enticed her in a soothing voice.

"I'm coming," she said, straining forward. Her foot took another step. She needed rest—eternal rest. Only then could she truly find peace and comfort in the arms of her dead husband.

Chapter Four

Violence Settles Nothing

The Crown & Cushion in Millgate filled with union members having a drink before the evening meeting. William entered and ordered an ale, looking forward to a slight reprieve after a long day's work. After taking a sip, he noticed his brother, Hugh, talking with Billy Saunders, the union treasurer. Curious about their intense conversation, he wandered over to eavesdrop. When they saw him approach, their mouths clamped shut.

"Hugh, Billy," William said in greeting.

"How's Mam?" Hugh asked.

"The same." William looked at them suspiciously. "So tell me, Billy, as treasurer, how much are we paying for bodily harm these days?"

A nervous laugh escaped his throat. "Oh, the sundry expense entry runs about ten or more pounds if we hire a professional."

"A bit much to throw a few punches, don't you think?" William snidely remarked.

"Often enough it's more than a few punches," his brother said. "Might as well add a kick or two." Hugh cried out a robust laugh, and Billy joined in.

Not agreeing to the humor, William changed the direction of the conversation. "What's on the agenda tonight?"

Billy lowered his speech and leaned toward him. "Problems with Stockport crossing lines."

"I was afraid of that," William remarked. "Anybody looked into that warehouse job I'm doing on Church Street? Bailey and I were thinking they might be Stockport bricks."

"Not sure if the delegates determined they are one of them, but there are other jobs in town they know about."

"Hope not. Hate to see all that hard work I've been doing the past week destroyed." William took a gulp of ale.

"Who you working for these days?" Billy inquired.

"Ashworth Brothers Building Works. Took the job when I heard they got the contract for the new warehouse. They were looking for bricklayers. Steady work for now." He hesitated for a moment. "Damn foreman is a slave driver, but most are anyway."

"They're still talking about building a new town hall," Hugh remarked. "It would mean plenty of work for years to come."

"Talking," William said. "They're always talking but never doing. It will take another ten committees and twenty town hall meetings for those politicians to come to a decision."

Bailey's brow rose at the comment, and he said with a snicker, "I bet you'd make a good politician who'd get the job done. You talk a fine discourse with all that education you got."

"I doubt the public would vote for a common laborer, though I dare say I'd like to try my hand at it one day," William mused aloud.

"That's where we differ," Hugh interjected. He reached over and gave William a strong pat on the back. "He's the conservative of the family, and I'm the liberal. He's the brains; I'm the brawn. We've never seen eye to eye on politics or religion, and I doubt we ever will."

"Don't seem like it's affected your relationship," Billy remarked, glancing back and forth at the two.

"We tolerate one another." William smirked, thinking it a half lie. The number of rows they had got louder and more frequent.

Hugh creased his lips at his snide remark. After setting the glass down on the bar, he gestured toward the door. "Better head for the public house and get a good seat."

William and Billy followed behind, and they walked a few yards down the road. They threaded their way through the crowd and found empty chairs. Usually two hundred union members from Manchester attended once a fortnight in summer and once a month in the winter. Charles Harrison was the current president of the union and called the meeting to order at half past eight.

"Take your places," his voice boomed across the hall. "There's much to discuss."

The wooden chairs creaked under the weight of the men as everyone sat down. Some who came too late to find a chair stood along the sidelines. William sat with Hugh, while Billy went up front to sit by the president and secretary, who had his book open to take the minutes.

After formally calling the meeting to order,

Harrison stood before the assembly. "We have a lot to discuss tonight, so let's have an quiet meeting and keep the shouting to a minimum."

The crowd let out a low grumble because most meetings resulted in yelling matches when the discontented attendees spouted their disputes. William settled in for the next hour, crossing his arms in front of his chest. Unions had their purposes to an extent, but William didn't always agree with their tactics on how the leaders ran things. Harrison continued with a booming voice that echoed in the large hall.

"As you all know, the society claims an extent of four miles round Manchester city lines in every direction. That's a hundred and twenty square miles, lads, as our district where no bricks are to be made except by Manchester union men. Neither are any bricks to be used in construction except those made in the district." He raised his voice. "Once again, we have Stockport crossing the district lines and slipping in bricks made by their nonunion workers who were hired by certain master brickmakers. These bricks are sold at a lower price, and contractors purchase them to save money. It's time we put a stop to this practice once and for all!"

"Hear, hear!" Men in the assembly shouted their agreement with such a roar, the floor vibrated. A few stood up and displayed their displeasure with gestures of raised fists. After the initial comment, they settled back down in their chairs. William glanced at Hugh, who looked edgy, and then braced himself for the evitable recommendation.

"Now we have proof," Harrison confirmed in a

firm tone, "from our own delegates they have seen the practice. We have followed the carters and watched where the bricks have been delivered. We've also sternly warned those knobsticks to cease their work, or they'd been losing more than their jobs."

"Teach 'em a lesson!" a voice called out.

Suddenly Hugh jumped to his feet and yelled above the audience. "I make a motion our enforcement council take action as they see fit."

"I second that motion," Steve Brown replied, rising as well.

William knew Steve to be one of the regular tyrants of the union who would see to it personally someone would pay. About to burst if he didn't speak, William stood up. Hugh spun his head and shot him a disgruntled look.

"I agree we need to impose the society's rules," he called out loud to be heard over the rumbling voices. "But I don't agree anybody gets bodily harmed as a result. Already the newspapers are calling us despots in our class for the outrages committed by the union." A moan thundered through the crowd.

"What do you suggest we do, Leighton?" Bailey, his coworker, bellowed. "Invite 'em for tea and ask 'em kindly to cease breaking the rules?"

"Perhaps we should bake scones," another called out in amusement.

The audience burst into a flurry of laughter, but William rejected their humiliation.

"I'm saying that diplomacy might be a new skill we should learn." The boom of laughter increased as well as the naysayers who threw curses in his direction.

Hugh tugged at William's sleeve. "Sit down, you fool," he growled. "You're gonna get yourself beat up in an alley."

As the members continued to guffaw, he sat down but boiled inwardly at their blind-sighted stupidity.

"Now, now, men," Harrison said, attempting to settle the ruckus. "We all got our opinions as Mr. Leighton so eloquently expressed. As a member, he has the right to speak, but we don't have to agree." After a few minutes, the crowd quieted. "The motion has carried, and we'll decide what needs to be done. If any of you want to make a few extra pounds, come see me after the meeting."

The invitation to be one of the thugs had gone out to the members. Anywhere from ten to twenty pounds would be split between the gang. William presumed they'd show up one dark night with coat collars above their ears, masks over faces, carrying sticks, shovels, or spade handles as weapons. He overheard that a few union members even brought single-barreled pistols. One of these days, somebody was going to get killed.

"Next order of business. We've started a fund to help defend those that may be arrested because of our enforcement duties. As you are aware, we've already defended a few of our union lads. Unions contribute for the defense and attorney fees to an amalgamated union fund. We've been using some money to defend Higgins for getting caught destroying bricks and a brickmaking machine at Lawson's yard."

William sat quietly for the remainder of the meeting, taking in the other complaints of supposed infractions in the district. Perhaps he would be good at something different from sitting in a chair at these meetings. No one appeared to give a damn what he had to say. The gatherings had become a waste of time as far as he was concerned.

An hour later, it finally concluded, and the members slowly left the public hall. A few men shot him resentful glances as they passed by and ran into him with their shoulders to make a point. Hugh acted irritated at him for giving his opinion, scowling as they made their way outdoors. When they did, he pulled William aside by the arm and shoved him against the building.

"You're only going to make enemies," he gruffly said, pointing his finger in his face. "Best to keep your mouth shut if you don't agree with the union's business. Nobody is going to listen to you anyway."

Pushed to his limit, William wiggled his body past Hugh and stood his ground in front of him. It didn't matter that he was a mere five feet eight inches compared to his brother's six-foot-two stance. He had bullied him as a child, and William wasn't about to let him intimidate him physically as an adult.

"Yes, God forbid, any civility comes out of these meetings. There isn't a soul that knows a damn thing about negotiation or diplomacy." He glowered at Hugh. "Don't you give a damn that history will record us as a bunch of terrorists, bullying our way through society? They call us animals of our class, and we eagerly act like jackasses."

Hugh's nostrils flared, and his veins bulged in his neck. "You're so bloody high and mighty with all your lofty ideals. Where in the hell did you come up with your nonsense?" He shoved his face in William's a few inches away. "Is it because our papa let you learn to read and write while I broke me back in the fields digging clay?"

"I'm thankful I had the opportunity," William replied, laced with irritation. "There's no shame in learning."

"Oh, I see. You're better than me because I have to make me mark on a piece of paper. I don't talk with 'em big words like you." He raised his voice, pulling his nostrils up in anger. "Who gives you the right to be the judge of us all?"

Hugh shook his fist at him as if he'd beat him to a pulp if he had the chance. It would be foolish to attempt to talk sense into his liberal-minded sibling.

"You and I will never see eye to eye." William reacted, shoving past him. "Why don't you go see Harrison and put your name in the hat as the next intimidator to make a few extra pounds since you look as if you'd enjoy beating the hell out of someone. It will help you focus your anger elsewhere."

Although rage boiled beneath the surface of his snide remarks, William, unlike his brother, didn't act on every heated emotion with a violent act. "I'm done talking," he gruffly replied.

William stormed off into the night, walking the dark streets back to his residence. A few of the cotton mills must have let out late as the roads were crowded with workers making their way home through the gas-lighted streets. The fleeting thought of a disgruntled union member following him raised the hair on the back of his neck. He wouldn't put it past some overly zealous idiot to jump him and give him a fist or two for having an opinion that differed from his. Why violence always had to be the reaction to everything made no sense whatsoever to William. Trying to live a peaceable life in an industrialized city, teaming with business, poverty, and dirt hadn't been the best place to hope for something better in life.

By the time he arrived, it was nine thirty, and the worry about his mother returned. He had departed at six o'clock that morning, leaving her alone in an empty house with her thoughts and melancholy.

As he approached, he saw no light through the window and wondered if she had retired for the evening. She had been sleeping more than usual, and he attributed her low spirits as the incentive to escape with her head on a pillow.

He entered through the door and stumbled into the darkness, fumbling to find the oil lamp and matches. Not wanting to wake his mother, he quietly set on fire the wick and increased the light. It took a few moments for his eyes to adjust as he glanced around. He half expected to see her sitting in a chair in the dark like other nights. Instead, it was empty, so he quietly ascended the staircase to the room they shared for sleep.

He rounded the corner toward the door, and the usual floorboards under his feet creaked beneath each step. Rather than call her name and wake her, he pushed open the barrier and stuck his head around the corner, expecting to see her on the mattress sound asleep. As he lifted the oil lamp higher, it illuminated the interior. To his utter horror, his mother hung limply against the far wall. She had taken one of his leather belts, wrapped it around her neck, and attached the buckle to a large nail overhead. He hastily set down the light on a nearby table and ran to her side.

"Mam, what have you done?" he wailed. When he touched her flesh, the coldness ran through his veins like ice. She had been dead for hours. Reaching above her head, he unhooked the end of the belt buckle and removed the strangling apparatus from around her throat and threw it across the room in anger.

"Oh, Mam, why? I told you we'd take care of you," he screamed. William clutched her in his arms and gawked at her contorted expression on her face. Her neck, black and blue from the belt, had choked the life from her body.

"Oh, Lord, forgive her," he cried, burying his head against hers. "She deserves heaven, not hell." His hand stroked her hair from her face, and he kissed her gently on her cold forehead, rocking her stiff body back and forth in his arms.

Violence had been the theme of the day. Violence to others and violence to self.

"Peace be with you, Mam," he whispered brokenhearted at the outcome of it all. "Peace be with you."

Chapter Five

An Unsound Mind

The week that followed, William and Hugh pushed aside their differences for the sake of their mother. A swift inquest the day after her death held a verdict of self-hanging while in the state of an unsound mind. The coroner released her body for burial.

As if their sorrow hadn't been enough to bear, they discovered they could not bury Martha in the same cemetery where their father had been laid to rest because it was consecrated ground. Instead, Father John Booker of Saint George's Church, where William attended, informed him that she must be buried on the north side of the church in an unmarked grave and could not be given the privilege of a proper funeral. The curate would attend for support, but no words would be recited from the *Book of Common Prayer*. The church deepened the wound of his loss.

When Hugh heard of it, he flew into a rage. "Where are the good folks of your parish now?" he mocked. "They deny your giving Mam a proper burial. Hypocrites they are—all of 'em."

"It's canon law." William weakly defended them but had hoped since he attended faithfully each Sunday that the vicar would give him an exception.

Instead, the church stood firm in his resolve not to stray. A part of William understood, but inwardly he resented his mother being treated as a lost soul not worthy of any honor in her death. As the inquest said, she was of unsound mind and surely God granted her mercy.

When they arrived for her burial, the plot lay open and her wood coffin had been lowered into the hole. An embankment of dirt sat alongside. In the far north corner of the churchyard, her grave lay next to a few babies that had died without being baptized.

Eliza brought a handful of field flowers. They had left Margaret with the neighbors rather than bringing her along. Hugh's face contorted with grief, and William struggled not to cry in the presence of family. The curate arrived with no prayer book in hand and stood nearby.

"I'm here to give you support at this dark hour," he announced. "As the vicar informed you, the church cannot grant any readings. May God have mercy on her soul."

"Do you believe in mercy?" William pointedly inquired, narrowing his eyes.

"Well... Well, of course I do." He stumbled over his words. "However, in this case—"

"In this case what?" Hugh bellowed. "She's burning in hell?" He took an angry step in the curate's direction. "You get the hell out of here! We'll bury her ourselves."

Defiant as Hugh's words, William pulled out his private prayer book and held it in his shaky hands. He glared at the man. "You can go," he said. "We'll give her the prayers she deserves."

He turned around and stomped toward the church. Hugh lowered his voice to a raspy whisper. "Get on with it, brother."

William opened the book, flipped to a dog-eared page he had marked, and read the text. Afterward, he finished with the final recitation.

"We commit our mother's body to the ground. Earth to earth, ashes to ashes, dust to dust; in the sure and certain hope of the resurrection to eternal life, through our Lord Jesus Christ."

They each grabbed a handful of dirt and let it slip through their fingers onto the wooden box. Eliza tossed the flowers on top.

Hugh's voice trembled. "I should have done what you said, William. I should have took her to me house. She'd still be alive today."

"Not your fault," William replied. His eyes moist with tears held no animosity toward his brother. "All that matters now is that she's at peace and with father."

"Holding our son in their arms too," Eliza added somberly.

Hugh turned away, struggling to keep his emotions in check. The gloomy day with gray clouds threatened rain.

"We best be getting back, Eliza," he said with a tremor in his voice. "Margaret will need feeding soon."

"Yes, of course." She turned toward William and gave him a quick hug.

"I'm so sorry for your loss. If you need anything, don't be shy. Promise?"

William nodded his head affirmatively.

"Brother, who is that lady?" Hugh asked, glancing toward the church. "She's been watching us all along."

He glimpsed in the direction and recognized the woman but didn't know her name. "I believe she's the niece of Father Booker. He took her into his home last year. Something about both her parents being dead."

"She's fine-looking," Hugh said. "You should go talk to her."

"What for?" He scowled.

Hugh gawked at Eliza. "He says what for? Can you believe how daft he can be at times?"

Eliza chuckled. "It wouldn't hurt you, William, to find a nice lady. You could use the company now."

"Oh, go." He waved them off. "Stop badgering me about women." He rolled his eyes as he mocked their voices. "You need to get married, William. You should have children, William."

"Give him a month or two," Hugh said to Eliza. "We can start playing matchmaker."

They walked away, and William shrugged off their comment. He turned and looked at the coffin but couldn't move. It was as if his feet sank into the earth, preventing him from leaving his mother behind in the cold grave.

"I miss you already, Mam. Don't know what I'll do with myself now." The answer came to mind in one word—work. His life had been consumed with work, so how did Hugh expect him to find a lady friend?

"Excuse me."

A female voice came from behind him. He turned around and faced the vicar's niece.

"Please forgive my intrusion," she said kindly. "I apologize for interrupting you at what must be a difficult time.”

Surprised at the salutation, William thought her voice sounded like an angel’s—soft and comforting.

“No problem, miss. I was just about to leave.” Suddenly William wanted to run from the churchyard. He glanced back and forth, looking for an escape route. He wasn’t good at talking with women. They made him nervous.

“Well, I’m the vicar’s niece. My name is Mary Booker.” She glanced down at the grave. “I wish to offer my sincere condolences at the loss of your mother and apologize that my uncle can be such a stick-in-the-mud when it comes to rules.”

“Thank you for your kind words,” William responded, nodding his head. Not sure what else she wanted, he took a step backward.

“I have experienced what it’s like to lose a parent. My mother and father are both dead. That’s why I’m with uncle now. He’s housing me until I can get on my feet and get a room at a boarding house.”

It was apparent she wanted to carry on a conversation, but his dry mouth felt like it had been stuffed with cotton.

“Pleasure… A pleasure to meet you, miss.”

“Oh, I’m rambling.” She scrunched her shoulders together. “I’ve seen you at service and wanted to greet you, but we hadn’t been properly introduced.” She lowered her head, and a slight blush tinted her cheeks. “I hope you don’t think me terribly forward for approaching you by myself. My uncle would be sorely displeased if he discovered that I had.”

Something about her demeanor and voice made her sound and look like a fine lady of breeding. No doubt, she had been educated and could read and write like him.

For the first time in his life, he sensed intrigued about a female. She had brown hair with hazel eyes. Wispy curls cascaded down the back of her head while the rest of her shiny locks were tucked underneath a modest hat. Her facial features were pleasant to look upon though he wouldn't term her a great beauty. Of course, with his overbearing nose that ran in the family, he wasn't a great looker either. Even more appealing was her height that did not reach his short stature.

Two men approached carrying shovels. "You done here? We got work to do."

Immediately the sound of their voice irritated William. Their tone and physical stance reeked of disrespect. He concluded they would bury his mother while making jokes about her demise. He would have none of it.

"Give me a shovel. I'll do it," he said, reaching out to take it from the gravedigger.

"Suit yourself," he replied, shoving it in his direction. "Just lean it by the tree over there when you're done." He handed William the spade, glanced at Miss Booker, and left.

William turned to her and excused himself. "Thank you your condolences. As you can see, I have work to do." William slipped out of his worn frock coat and laid it on a clean patch of grass. As he rolled up his sleeves, Miss Booker looked at him forlornly.

"Do take care of yourself," she said in parting. "Looks like it might rain."

"Don't you worry about me," he replied. "I'm good

at taking care of myself." He didn't know why he said the rebuking remark. The disappointment in the lady's eyes became visible, but William had other things on his mind besides women.

"Goodbye." Her voice quavered. She meandered slowly toward the vicarage, appearing downcast with a lowered head.

Not much could be done about it as he thrust the shovel into the dirt. "Sorry, Mam," he said, thinking of her cold body inside the coffin. "It's time to say goodbye." When he tipped the spade, the first mound of dirt slowly trickled down upon the coffin, covering the flowers that Eliza had left on top. He stood there for a few minutes staring at it when a scripture floated through his mind.

"For what is your life? It is even a vapor, that appeareth for a little time and then vanisheth away."

As he tossed dirt into the grave, each haul felt as if he smothered the vapor of his mother's life. A raindrop splattered on his cheek. He didn't mind the rain. With a wet face, no one would notice the tears as the two droplets mingled together. William loathed showing weakness of character, but after all, he was burying the woman who birthed him into this world.

By the end of the arduous task, he stood soaked to the bone. The skies opened a deluge, but at least his mother had been buried with dignity. It brought him peace to honor her to the end.

William leaned the shovel against a nearby tree and stood underneath it for protection from the rain. His suit coat lay in a muddy patch, and he was chilled to the bone. To his surprise, he noticed the vicar coming his way with an open umbrella. He could have punched the man to rid himself of his lingering anger. When he arrived, he spoke.

"Mary told me you'd be out here in the rain, William."

"Couldn't leave my mother to the diggers," he replied unashamedly.

"Well, why don't you come back to the vicarage for a spell and sit in front of the fire and have a cup of hot tea? You'll catch your death like that in your current state. I don't wish to be burying another."

The offer sounded inviting, but it meant seeing Mary. He wasn't quite sure if he would be up to pleasantries. Regardless, when another shiver wiggled down his spine, he relented.

"Sounds good to me."

William picked up his soggy suit coat and followed the vicar. No doubt, Hugh would encourage him to take an interest in the young lady. Perhaps he would—perhaps he wouldn't.

Chapter Six

The Ways of Women

William huddled underneath the umbrella shared by the vicar. By the time they reached the house, his shoes squished like a soaked sponge. They entered the foyer, and Mary greeted them with a broad smile.

"Here's a towel," she offered, handing it to him. His wet hair dripped in his face, so he took it without complaint and dabbed his skin.

"Thank you, miss."

"Now listen here, William," the vicar ordered. "You take off those wet clothes, and we'll put them over a chair by the fireplace to dry."

"Well, um…" William didn't quite know what to say, thinking he'd be down to his drawers in front of Mary. The vicar laughed when he saw the awkwardness on his face.

"Follow me upstairs. I've got an old pair of pants and a cotton shirt you can put on in the meantime."

Relieved at the suggestion, William followed him to the bedchamber. After rifling through his closet, he selected brown pants and a white cotton shirt.

"We're not much different in size. These should do in a pinch." He laid them down at the end of the bed. "Brings those wet things downstairs when you're done."

After closing the door, William glanced around the room. He eyed the bed and wanted to crawl under the covers. It was an actual canopy bed on a wooden platform, with a lovely print quilt and fluffy pillows. It put to shame the two old mattresses he and his mam had slept on perched on a wobbly metal frame about ready to break. The window overlooked the gardens out back, and William fought jealousy about the accommodations the church had provided. It only reminded him of the poverty of his class.

He stripped his body of the wet garments and slipped into the borrowed clothing. They fit well enough. Barefoot, with his wet stockings stuffed in his shoes, he made his way downstairs with the rest of his attire over his arm. Ashamed of his ugly feet, he paid no attention to them so Mary wouldn't notice their disgusting appearance. He felt naked in front of the young lady.

Two wooden table chairs had been placed with their backs toward the fireplace. William draped his shirt, pants, and suit coat on the back. He set down his shoes on the hearth floor and laid out his stockings that had holes in the toes. The warmth of the fire chased away the chill in his body.

"Thank God the heat spell is done. The rain is a welcome reprieve," the vicar said. "Doubt I would have built a fire a month ago."

"Yes, indeed. It's been unbearably hot." William took an empty chair and sat down.

Mary entered the room, carrying a tray, holding a pot of tea, cups, and saucers. A few biscuits were on a plate. She set it down on a table in front of them.

"Ah, thank you, Mary."

"You're welcome, uncle," she replied, glancing at William and smiling again. Her eyes sparkled.

The vicar picked up the pot and put the tea strainer above the cup. "How do you take your tea, William?"

"A bit of milk, vicar," he replied.

"No need to call me vicar. I much prefer John." The vicar passed the hot brew to him, but he held it until others were served.

"Drink up and get some warmth inside you," the stern voice of his host ordered.

Mary's eyes widened. "Uncle," she said, pulling her mouth to one side. "I'm sure he'll drink when he's ready."

William took a sip and enjoyed the warmth.

John cleared his throat. After taking a quick sip of his tea, he spoke solemnly.

"I want personally to apologize for being unable to accommodate your request for your mother's funeral."

William sat up and listened, irritated he had broached the subject. He didn't care to discuss the matter. Nevertheless, if the man wished to apologize for hurting the family, he would pay attention.

"The bishop caught wind of the incident after reading of it in the newspaper and came to see me straightaway, demanding that I remain faithful to canon law should you choose to bury your mother here."

"I'm not fond of the bishop," Mary interjected. "He reminds me of a tyrant."

"Mary, please," the vicar said in a scolding tone.

"Sorry," she sheepishly replied. "But he is." She took a sip of tea with a mischievous smirk on her face.

"I won't deny my heart broke at the decision," William admitted. "My brother, Hugh, was furious, and it did no good for him either since he hates the church." William softened his tone. "No matter. Mother is buried now, and I am content that she is at peace."

"I'm glad to hear of it," Mary remarked. "God is merciful."

"Yes, yes, I agree," John replied. "The Almighty chooses mercy instead of judgment."

The room grew silent as each fell into their own thoughts, sipping tea and watching the crackling fire dry William's clothes. Tomorrow he would return to work. Perhaps it would help to keep busy and his grief-filled thoughts elsewhere.

"So what are your plans now, young man?"

A bit confused about the question, he looked straight-faced at the vicar. "Not quite sure what you mean."

"About living alone," he said. "What are you twenty-five or twenty-six? A lad of your caliber should be settled down by now with a wife and children." John snickered. "What's taking you so long?"

A nervous chuckle left William's throat. Mary's cheeks flushed, and she pulled her lingering gaze elsewhere.

"Well, to be quite honest, sir, I'm not sure how to go about courting the ladies." Nervous about his inexperience, he lowered his eyes. "I can handle a red brick quite well, but I don't have the finesse to handle delicate females, I'm afraid."

"Oh, I see." John cackled. "Shy, are we?"

"Uncle, can't you see you're making Mr. Leighton uncomfortable with all your prodding?" Mary gave his arm a slight poke with her fingertip.

"Ah, now my niece here," he added, "she'd make a fine wife, but she's a bit assertive if you get my drift." He pushed away her finger, which Mary withdrew. She folded her hands in her lap, looking mortified by avoiding eye contact.

"Well, I'll be frank," William replied for her sake. "I'm not in a position to take on a wife. Need to save some money, be settled in a decent house. I got plans, you see."

The vicar leaned forward in his direction. "Plans, you say? Like what?"

William cleared his throat and took the time to formulate a response. He didn't want to sound like an utter fool spouting off ideas, but he had dreams that went beyond mortar and bricks.

"I hope someday to be a master brickmaker and employ a fine crew of brick setters myself. I've mastered the art, but I see new inventions being talked about like brickmaking machines." He started to get excited at the thought of the innovation, and he became more animated in his demeanor. "Can you imagine how much quicker we can produce quality bricks if a machine does it?"

"Hmm," the vicar mused. "From what I've read in the newspaper, isn't there opposition from the union about machine-made bricks being used in Manchester?"

The union—the unavoidable barrier that stifled

creativity at every turn. William subscribed to its usefulness on some levels. However, its leaders were not progressive thinking folk and vehemently resisted change. They made it difficult for anybody who wanted to better themselves and had caused plenty of would-be masters to go out of business.

"You are right," William agreed. "They don't understand the benefits of developments, but someday I hope they will come around."

"You have grand ambitions, Mr. Leighton," John mused aloud. "I believe if you put your mind to it, you just might succeed with the Lord's help."

William glanced at Mary, who intently observed his every move, clinging to his words as well. Her eyes studied him as if she were attempting to ascertain if he could make something of himself or not.

"Mary is eager to leave and go out on her own, but I think she needs to stay with me a bit longer. She's got plans too, so she tells me."

The statement piqued William's interest. "What sort of plans do you have?"

"Oh, they're just silly dreams," she said, lowering her head.

"No dreams are silly, miss." William pressured her for an answer. "I want to know about your dreams. I've told you mine."

She lifted her head with renewed confidence. "I would love to have a millinery store. Hats are my passion, you see."

"Ah, hats." William shook his head in agreement. "Women do need hats, and I'm sure there would be plenty of business."

"Hats." The vicar pulled his mouth to the side.

"Mary needs to get married, have babies, and keep a home. Business is no place for a woman." He pointed to the Bible sitting on a side table. "The first book of Timothy clearly says that younger women should marry, bear children, guide the house, and give none occasion to the adversary to speak reproachfully. That should be her goal."

John's singsong voice turned stern, and each word like a hatchet chopped Mary's dream of a hat shop to pieces. William didn't personally know of any women in business, but if she had hopes of bettering herself, he would support her wholeheartedly.

"Her father and mother," the vicar continued, "made sure she had an education for reading and writing. Girls don't need to be schooled either. Waste of time. They need to help their mothers care for the home."

William couldn't argue the point, frankly. He did have the opinion that women were not necessarily scholars by any means. "I can read and write," he announced. Mary's eyes fixated on him, and he gazed in return. "My father was a poor bricklayer too, and my brothers didn't have the chance for schooling. I got to go long enough to learn before being put in the fields to dig for clay."

"Well, good for you." John drank the last of his tea while Mary rose to her feet and walked over to his clothes. She rearranged them a bit.

"They are nearly dry, Mr. Leighton."

"Well, I should finish the tea and have one of those delicious-looking biscuits and be on my way. Work comes early in the morning," he replied.

An insistent knock came to the door, and the vicar

rose to answer it. "Now who in the world could that be?"

He left the room and stepped into the foyer. William took advantage of the moment alone with Mary.

"I think you have a grand idea," he said. "Marriage and babies can wait until you're ready."

"It's a silly notion, I realize."

The vicar stepped back into the room. "I apologize, but I must be going. It appears Mr. Olsen is about to leave his earthly body and join the Lord. His wife is asking me to come."

"Then let me swiftly change and leave too." William knew it wouldn't be proper for him to stay with Mary in the house alone. He set down his teacup, grabbed his clothes from off the chair, and ran upstairs to change. They were a bit damp but much better than before. When he returned, the vicar looked anxious to leave.

"Thank you for your hospitality," William said. "I appreciate the tea, biscuits, and company." He smiled warmly at Mary.

"Goodbye, Mr. Leighton." Her voice sounded laced with disappointment.

He stepped out the door and thanked John once more. The rain had subsided, and the vicar speedily followed Mrs. Olsen back to her residence. William wanted to walk to the grave and say a few more words to his mother but then decided not to. It was time to go home and make decisions about the future.

A quick glance back at the vicarage revealed Mary parting the curtains and looking at him. William considered her subtle actions, wondering if she had taken a fancy to him. If so, it would be the first time any woman had taken note of him. He was unsure what if anything he should do about it now. She was a smart young lady with a bit of gumption, and William found that likable. For a second he stared at her in return, nodded, and then turned to leave. The day had been filled with sorrow and surprise, and he wondered what tomorrow would hold.

Chapter Seven

MORE HARM THAN GOOD

William woke the following morning with his eyes gazing at his mother's empty bed. The surroundings were void of human presence—not even a wisp of a ghost remained in his midst. He wasn't sure how long he'd be able to handle the solitude before going mad. At least his days were long on the job, and after arriving home, he could sleep away the loneliness. As far as food, a loaf of bread, some cheese, boiled potatoes, and dried red herring would be enough to fill his belly.

He rose, splashed his face with water, and combed his unruly hair. He pushed the strands underneath a cap and made a mental note that he needed to visit the washhouse for a public bath in the next week. When he headed out the door, the Manchester air lay heavy as a cloud from the factories spewing out their morning smoke.

The walk to the job site invigorated him somewhat until he halted and gawked at the scene of destruction. Piles of bricks lay broken in heaps, and the newly constructed walls of the warehouse had been pushed over where the mortar had not yet dried. It appeared as if a gang of sledgehammer-armed men arrived in the dark to do their evil deeds, laying ruin to all their work the weeks before. What they could not tumble over in heaps, they smashed and destroyed. Weeks of hard toil lay in shambles. The work crew huddled around Thorpe, who held a paper in his hand.

"What's going on?" William asked, approaching and standing by the rest of the men. He glimpsed at Bailey, who sported a smug look on his face.

"We'll have to let you all go, I'm afraid."

"Go?" Bailey screeched. "What the bloody hell do you mean? There's plenty of work here to rebuild."

"You would think so, but Mr. Ashworth lost the contract on the warehouse construction," Thorpe announced. "Whatever union thugs did here the other night didn't hurt just him but you as well. You stupid bastards," he mumbled.

"I don't understand," William asked. Anger gnawed at his gut.

"What's there to understand, Leighton? The owner who contracted the work for this warehouse doesn't have the funds to purchase the bricks to replace the damaged lot. Instead, the man is filing for bankruptcy. Ashworth lost the contract and could go out of business, and now you jolly lads are out of a job. No other contracts are pending to put you on, so we're letting you go."

"What did I tell you, Bailey?" William shouted in ire, turning his narrowed eyes upon him. "When are those union hooligans going to get some brains? Did you tell them these were nonunion, nondistrict bricks?"

"Well, I..." Bailey stumbled at his words, rubbing the back of his neck.

"You fucking idiot," Thorpe yelled. "You might as well have taken a pistol and shot yourself in the foot."

"Well, did the contractor bring 'em in from Stockport?" Bailey pressured the foreman, trying to save face.

"He got twenty thousand bricks from Stockport because the brickmaker we were using couldn't meet the quota in time."

"What are we supposed to do now?" Johnson asked. "I got kids to feed and a baby on the way." He ran his fingers through his hair in frustration and fear.

"Well, I wrote down some names of a few contractors who are hiring. Brickyards are looking for workers in the field, and some master brickmakers need help." He thrust the paper in Leighton's direction.

"Why don't you help the lads here figure it out? I don't have the stomach to deal with this either. You're not the only one out of work." He shoved his hands in his pocket and nodded at the crew. "Good luck, lads."

William snarled in Bailey's face. His hands tingled. "If I was a violent man, I'd punch you in the jaw."

"Me dad's gonna whoop me if I'm not workin'," Teddy said, looking like a scared rabbit. "He'll stick me in a cotton mill for sure now. I hate 'em places." His voice trembled.

The men on the crew drew close to William, waiting to hear names on the list. "Since you got us in this mess, Bailey, you can read it." He shoved the list in Bailey's direction, but he didn't take it.

"You're the only one here who can read, Leighton," he sheepishly replied. "You do it."

Lowering his eyes to the paper, William read the list of five companies that Thorpe had scratched out on paper. He looked at the crew size and the possible openings and realized there were more men than jobs—and he was one of them.

He had just lost his mother, and now he was unemployed. Someone might as well have punched him in the gut. Dreadful thoughts of homelessness and starvation wiggled through his brain like snakes. William shook them off and handed the paper to Teddy.

"You take this home to your dad and let him have a look. Can he read?"

"Don't think so, but I can remember the names. He isn't gonna like it though 'cause he's been out of work too. I'll end up going with Mam to the mill with me brothers."

William reached out his hand and playfully rustled the boy's hair. "I'm sure you'll do just fine. You're a good worker, Teddy."

The men started to meander away from the site with slumped shoulders. Some demolition crew would come and clean up the mess. Maybe they'd bring in men from the workhouse to do the dirty job. As long as he didn't end up there with them, he'd persevere and move on.

"Well, Bailey, good luck, chump. You shot yourself in the foot all right." He waved at him and walked away. "See you around at the meetings."

"Bye, William," he mumbled, glancing at the broken heaps of bricks.

For a second, William thought he'd get an apology from Bailey, but none came. The union didn't care as long as they kept enforcing the regulations that were supposed to protect the members. It didn't matter who suffered—members, master brickmakers, contractors, or businessmen.

William wandered back home in no hurry to return to an empty room. He stuck his hand in his pocket and counted what he had left from last week's thirty shillings of pay. Only fifteen remained, and rent would be due in another week. Without another mouth to feed, he might make rent and food. Clearly he was going to have to move out of the two-room row house and find something smaller to live but had no idea where to look.

A young lad in knickers stood on the corner, selling newspapers, and William purchased one to read the advertisements. He folded and tucked the paper under his arm and strode down the street. When he came to a pub, he halted before the doors. It wasn't the time to be spending money, but he needed a drink and headed for the bar. He ordered an ale, found a table, and sat down. After gulping the liquid to soothe his parched throat, he opened the daily news and began pursuing the jobs postings.

"Irish need not apply" appeared after a few advertisements. Prejudice never ended in some classes, and William passed by those because it irked him. Nothing of significance had been posted, and he folded the paper and tossed it on the tabletop in frustration. Grabbing his glass, he gulped the drink, mulling over his options while he stared out the window at the people. The street, choked with horses, carriages, omnibuses, and folks on foot all had somewhere to go except him. He pondered telling

Hugh of his predicament, but his brother possibly had agreed to or even participated in the destruction at his job site. The thought resurrected nothing but anger.

"Bloody idiot," he grumped. After he realized that his voice carried, he attempted to calm down and fingered his half-empty glass while scowling at the tabletop.

"Excuse me." A male voice addressed him.

William looked up and saw a tall, well-dressed man peering down at him, holding a glass of ale in his hand. Confused as to why he had stopped to address him, he replied.

"What can I do for you?" William asked.

"I couldn't help but notice you and wondered if you were a tradesperson—a bricklayer, perhaps."

Sure, he had his cap on, his dusty work clothes, a few dabs of dry mortar on his shirtsleeve that might have hinted at his occupation. Did it look that obvious? No doubt, the rough and cracked skin on his hands added to the suspicion. Slightly miffed, he got to his feet and addressed the stranger face-to-face.

"Yes, bricklayer," he answered, attempting to keep an ounce of pride in spite of his current predicament. "Is there something you want from me?" William's irritated tone exposed his sour mood.

"Well, yes, if you don't mind. I'd like to ask you some questions about your profession as well as your participation in the union—that is if you're a union man."

The man fidgeted, acting as if he had second thoughts for approaching. William's gruff responses probably gave him cause for concern. He couldn't help but wonder if the bloke worked at the newspapers, looking for a story on the recent outrages. At that moment, William had enough indignation in his soul to spew out a few details, so he decided to pursue the man's real intentions.

"Union man, yes. Have a seat," William said, pointing to the empty chair on the other side of his table. "What do you want to know?"

The man gave no hesitation and sat down like an eager dog, waiting for his meal. He took a sip of his ale, set the glass on the table, and looked at William curiously.

"You will perhaps think me daft," he began. "But I'm wondering about investing in the new brickmaking machinery. I'd like to start a business."

William's right brow rose in astonishment. He straightened his spine and leaned forward. "Business, you say? Good for you. If I had the means and opportunity, I start one myself as a master."

The stranger continued to look at him, eyeing William again with interest. "My father passed away recently and left me a bit of money," he admitted. The fingers of his hand turned around his glass, and he watched it make a circle before speaking again.

"Sorry to hear of your loss." William wanted to mention his mother, but he didn't see the point in bringing up her death.

"What do you think about these apparatuses?" he suddenly gushed forth.

Excited at the prospects of having an intelligent conversation about innovation, William replied.

"I've seen pictures of the Bradley & Craven brickmaking machinery. It's a marvel for sure but..."

His words trailed off because the union bitterly opposed the use of the machines.

"But what?"

"A lot of the union members are against the machines, and as you no doubt are aware, there have been attacks on brickmakers who use them."

"Yes, so I've heard." He scowled. The man lowered his head for a moment, crinkled his brow, and then thoughtfully spoke. "But if I hire union men to work for me, set up business on the outskirts of the city, and pay my subscription fees to the Brickmaker's Society, do you think they'll leave me in peace?"

William snickered at the idea. "Hard to say, mister..." They had been talking for a few minutes, and he didn't even know the stranger's name.

"Oh, sorry," the man said. "My name is Reggie Cooper." The gentleman introduced himself. "And you are?"

"William Leighton," he responded, reaching across the table to offer a handshake. "Pleasure to meet you." Mr. Cooper grabbed his hand and gave it a hearty, strong wobble in return.

It appeared to William that an opportunity might be presenting itself, so he pursued the conversation in an eager tone. "So what are your plans, if you don't mind me asking? If you can't sell the bricks in the Manchester district, what do you plan on doing with them?"

"I imagine there's a need for well-made bricks elsewhere outside the four-mile limit. Lots of housing going up these days in Broughton and beyond," he surmised. "If the city ever gets around to building the new town hall, there's going to be a huge demand.

Rumor has it brickmakers are struggling to make the quotas needed."

"The union can be impossible to deal with regrettably," William replied in a somber tone. He didn't wish to deter the man's ambitions, but he might as well tell him the truth of the situation. "Even members aren't immune from the consequences. I just lost my job at one of the sites that used out-of-district bricks on a new warehouse going up on Church Street."

Mr. Cooper's eyes widened and he leaned forward. "You mean the one that was damaged last night? I read about it in the newspapers this morning."

"I must have missed that article," William said, pushing the paper aside.

"Bloody shame, if you ask me." He shook his head, narrowing his eyes in concern.

"Damn so since my employer lost the contract and his money on the warehouse. He let the entire crew go this morning. I'm officially out of work." William snickered at the absurdity of the situation.

"Well, damn then," Mr. Cooper replied, taking a sip of his ale. William did as well as they both fell into a digestive moment of silence.

"Where are you contemplating starting your business?" William inquired.

"Broughton," he replied.

"You'll get flooded out in Lower Broughton if you set up shop there," William said.

"No, Higher Broughton. I've been in discussions with the landowners about renting some of their empty fields that provide a good source of clay."

"Have they agreed?"

"Yes, but we haven't settled on a price yet."

A bit envious that the man had the means to start a business, he kept his facial expression unresponsive. Since he had no one to leave him any inheritance, he could rule out that opportune chance in his lifetime.

"What about the site for the brickmaking? Have you settled on a location?"

"Yes, a half mile away there are some vacant buildings for rent that would suffice. There's enough room for the machinery, drying the bricks, the kiln, and storage."

William never considered himself cheeky enough to jump into prospects where he hadn't been asked, but desperation called for action. He had enough knowledge of the fields, brickmaking, and bricklaying to be of help to the man who seemed to have more business sense than brickmaking knowledge.

"Do you know much about the trade?" William asked, curious if he ever picked up a trowel himself.

"Can't say I do," Mr. Cooper replied. "Couldn't lay a brick in a straight line if I tried. Don't know anything about cotton either, but brickmaking seems to be a place to make money. I've been reading about various trades, trying to decide which one to make a go of it. If you look for a need to fill, it usually leads to success. My father dabbled in a bit of construction, so I am versed on how to go out and bid on jobs—that sort of thing."

The man appeared sincere enough and full of ambition. He looked to be in his midthirties, about William's height, and sported a dark head of hair and facial beard that had been well trimmed. He certainly could talk well enough with an education to back his endeavors.

"Obviously you don't know me, Mr. Cooper, but if you need help in this new endeavor of yours, I'd be more than happy to help you get it off the ground." William felt no shame in asking.

The man looked a bit surprised but didn't appear offended by his bold offer. "You got references, Leighton?"

He nodded his head affirmatively. "Yes, I have good references I can supply you when needed," he assured him. "I'm not a union troublemaker either. Don't adhere to the likes of violence in any form."

"No, you don't seem the kind from the few minutes I've spent with you. From what I hear, the union has been a troublemaker for you."

"Well, I attend the meetings and try to put some sense into their stubborn attitudes but don't get far."

They spent the next hour chatting about everything from the weather to politics. William enjoyed the man's company, and they mostly saw eye to eye on quite a few issues. Mr. Cooper told him a bit about his childhood and parents, but William had nothing of significance to share about his upbringing. When they had come to an end of their discussions, Mr. Cooper picked up his glass and downed the rest of his ale. He slipped his hand into his pocket, pulled out a calling card, and handed it to William.

"Here's my address, Leighton. Give me a month or so and then come to see me. I should be in a position to give you an update and let you know when I can bring on workers. There's a lot to be done, and it takes time to get the machine from the makers and have it delivered."

William took the card and noted the address. "I'll take you up on the offer, Mr. Cooper. It's been a pleasure talking to you."

They both stood to their feet and shook hands. "I hope you find work soon to tide you over until I figure out what I'm going to do. If you need something, contact me."

Surprised at the kind offer, William nodded. "Thank you. I will."

Mr. Cooper left the pub, and William shoved the card in his pocket. The day had started in disaster but appeared to be ending better than he expected. Regardless of what would become of Mr. Cooper and his new commercial endeavor, William needed to find work as soon as he could.

He swallowed the last drops of his drink and left the pub for home.

Chapter Eight

TAKING CARE OF OUR OWN

The bread was stale, the cheese moldy, and William's stomach growled to match his mood. He sat in the room lit only by the oil lamp and glanced around the empty surroundings. Nothing of value filled the place—an old wooden table and two chairs, an empty rocking chair of his mother's, a rickety chest of drawers, and a few utensils, dishes, and pots for cooking on the wood stove insert in the fireplace. The barrenness of the room played on the grief of his loss of companionship and livelihood. He let out a defeated sigh and lowered his head into his hands. The self-pity lasted but a second when a loud bang came at the door.

"Let me in," Hugh bellowed from the other side.

The timing of his brother's visit annoyed William. Regardless, he rose to his feet, walked to the door, and swung it open. Aggravated at the sight of him, William stood in the center of the doorway to prevent his entrance.

"I'm not in the frame of mind for visitors," he grimly stated.

"I couldn't care less," Hugh said, pushing past him. He nearly knocked him over. "If you think I'm going to let you gripe in here by yourself, you're a misguided sod."

William flung the door shut with a bang. "What do you want?" He scowled at Hugh standing before him in an intimidating stance, glancing around the room.

"I'm here on behalf of the union," he said, shoving his hand into his pants pocket. Hugh fiddled with coins and then brought out a handful of money. "Because of the recent events, it has been decided that the crew on your job would receive relief funds since the builder lost the contract."

"Is the union admitting wrongdoing?"

"Wrong?" Hugh clutched the money in his hand tight as if he had withdrawn the offer. "We did what was necessary to enforce the rules."

"Did you participate in the damage?" William advanced a step in his brother's direction. "Well, did you?"

"And what does that have to do with it if I did?" He scowled and thrust his hand in William's direction. "Here's three pounds for whatever you need until you can find another job."

Unable to tell by the look on Hugh's face if he had swung one of the sledgehammers, he glanced at his fist instead. If only he could refuse the money, his conscience would find relief but his belly would remain empty. Without rent, he'd be forced to slump over a rope line to find sleep in the doss house somewhere. Necessity urged him to calm the anger and swallow his pride. He held out his empty palm.

"Thank you," he said, lowering his voice.

Hugh's firm stance softened as he relaxed his shoulders in relief. "Good time not to be stubborn," he said, shoving the coins into William's empty palm. Afterward, he walked over and sat down in a chair by the table. "What are you going to do now?" he asked.

"Look for work," William replied. He resumed his seat and brushed the stale crumbs off the tabletop.

"Listen, William, I'm sorry it turned out this way. I know you don't agree with the union's tactics."

"You're right, I don't."

"On the other hand, this might be a good thing for you."

"How do you figure that?"

"You got ideas and ambitions," Hugh replied. "I got the burliness in the family, and you got the brains," he said, bellowing a husky laugh.

William snickered at Hugh's antics as he struck a muscular pose like a ring fighter. He'd probably do well in a fistfight, while he, on the other hand, would end up with a bloody nose and broken bones. After the levity settled down between them, he wanted to mention the happenchance meeting with Reggie Cooper. Bringing up the matter of buying a brickmaking machine would result in another spat. Without thinking straight, he gushed out the other issue.

"Talked to the vicar's niece," he said. When the words left his lips, Hugh perked up.

"You did? So when's the wedding?"

"Your wit is irksome." William flicked a few more crumbs off the tabletop to bide his time before giving Hugh the details.

"Well, what happened?" he pressed. "Spit it out."

"I stayed and filled Mam's grave by myself," he announced.

"Oh, for God's sake, Will. Why didn't you tell me you wanted to do that? I would have helped."

"You left, and the gravediggers came over to start the job. Didn't like their attitude, so I shooed them away and grabbed the shovel."

"Then what?"

"I started to fling dirt. What do you think?"

"I reckon you did. What else?"

"It started to rain, and by the time I was finished, I was drenched. The vicar came out with an umbrella and invited me back to his house for tea and to warm up."

"At times like these, I wish I had an ale," Hugh remarked. "Can't remember the last time we had such an engaging conversation about female folk."

William chuckled as he dreamed about Mary. She did bring a smile to his face, but now he doubted anything would come of it.

"I think she fancies me," he said in a morose tone of voice.

"You don't sound too excited about it." Hugh's enthusiasm deflated. "Why?"

"I'm in no position to support a wife." He crossed his arms, defying the idea. "Besides, I don't know the first thing about courting a woman or even touching one for that matter."

Naturally Hugh burst out in another booming laughter. William swore he blushed as heat rushed into his cheeks. It was the truth though. He'd never even kissed a woman and didn't think himself much of a romancer. After all, his life had been consumed with being an apprentice and finally becoming a journeyman at his trade. Afterward, taking care of his mother had also filled his life with responsibilities that gave no room for a lady friend. Yet he had to admit while sitting in the empty room that he disappeared into the drab surroundings, lost and lonely. He had to get out of it.

"You wanna know about women, I can teach you," Hugh said eager to share. "You'll love the warmth of her naked body and the smooth touch of her big tits." A roguish grin curled his lips. "Does the lass have big tits?"

William's eyes widened at Hugh's crass remark. In answer, he scowled but said nothing as he thought about Mary's well-endowed figure.

"Nothing like squeezing a woman's breast to make a man in the mood for love."

"All right, enough of that," William ordered. He put his hands over his ears. Hugh shook his head.

"You're gonna die a bachelor. I can see it now. By the time you get around to it, all the pretty women will be gone. There will be nothing to pick from but ugly spinsters."

His brother sounded serious. The thought of lying next to an ugly woman sent a shiver down his spine. He didn't know much about what lay under the skirt and what it had to offer, but men needed an agreeable face to look on to feel the need.

"Fine, I get the picture. Next time some lady fancies me, I'll pay more attention."

Steering the conversation elsewhere, William spoke.

"I'm moving from here, Hugh. No need to stay in this place. Surely I can find a decent room to rent."

"Well, get a job first," he advised. "No one will rent

to you if you're not working. They'll send you to the doss house for a straw hole or a rope."

William nodded his head. "True."

"I hear new estates are going up in Broughton," Hugh mentioned. "You should find out who's the master bricklayer on those jobs and see if you can't pick something up."

"Broughton?"

"Aye, rich merchants from outside the country have been settling there. Turks or something like that. Can you believe Turks in England? Don't they wear those funny turbans or something?"

William hesitated to correct Hugh's assumption. "I don't think they're Turks," he said. "Christians, I read in the papers, fleeing the Turks. They built a Greek Orthodox Church off New Bury Road."

"Go figure," Hugh responded, scratching his head. "Like you to set me straight since you can read about 'em things."

William's mind drifted elsewhere. "Would Eliza like any of Mam's things? There isn't much. Perhaps a few of her hats are still decent."

"No, I don't think so. You just give 'em to charity and be done with it."

Exhausted from the emotional day, William yawned.

"Well, I should be going," Hugh remarked, taking the hint.

"Thank the union officers for the handout," William stated. "It will keep me off the ropes at least."

"I'd give you me floor to sleep on, brother, before I'd let you visit one of those hellholes."

Hugh got up and walked toward the door. "Take

care. If you need anything, let me know."

"I will."

William watched Hugh walk down the street for a moment until he disappeared in the dark around the corner. He glanced about, and most folks had gone indoors for the night. The thought of doing so himself caused him to delay further. Indoors had memories of finding his mother dead with a belt around her neck, hanging from an old nail high in the wall. Since her death, he had pulled the damn thing out as he couldn't bear to look at it, but the image of her limp body remained in his mind. He needed to move.

William leaned against the doorjamb, inhaled the night air, wondering if Broughton's quality was any better. Most of Lower Broughton had been developed, but contractors avoided building there because the River Irwell was prone to flooding during the rainy season. He thought about checking out the potential clay fields that belonged to the local landowner, which Mr. Cooper mentioned. If he saw them firsthand, he could give the man his opinion on the matter the next time they met.

William yawned. Regardless of how empty and quiet the interior would be when he returned inside, he couldn't forgo sleep. After returning indoors, he closed the door behind him and found his way to bed.

Chapter Nine

LUCK OR FATE?

The next morning William made his way to Manchester town center and paid the fare to ride an omnibus to Broughton. He hadn't been in the region for some time and settled back to take in the view from his seat on top of the coach. The carriage traveled down Great Ducie Street that merged into New Bury Road, taking him farther away from the squalor of the neighborhood in which he lived.

They passed the workhouse, and he pondered the poor souls whose lives had been doomed to a wretched existence. William noted the irregular development after going by Strangeways. Lower Broughton passed on the left and Cheetham on the right. Eventually the carriage came to a stop nearing Higher Broughton. William saw the vast field that Mr. Cooper had mentioned, so he disembarked to take a closer look.

Across the street on New Bury Road, development had been evident, but to the right where he stood, large expanses of land stretched before him. From what Cooper mentioned, the landowner had kept a tight control of the development. Should he be able to lease the fields for brickworks, William agreed it would be a prime location.

As he glanced around the landscape and strolled through the locale, William had a gut sense that much could be accomplished in the vicinity. There existed ample room for growth. A few industrial factories, a dye works and print works, spotted the landscape, but no workhouses or slums were nearby. The smoke from the factories in Manchester was not as prevalent. He inhaled the air and savored the freshness.

Satisfied that the land would be suitable for Cooper's endeavor, William explored the streets. Content in his stroll, he came upon an area of residential construction that Hugh had mentioned. Terraced cottages with yards and individual grand residences were being constructed for the middle class who could afford better housing.

As he wandered by one construction location, he stopped and observed a crew hard at work. The brickwork was impeccable and detailed above the windows and doors, and William couldn't restrain himself from edging his way toward the site. The foreman, wearing a bowler hat, caught sight of him and drew near.

"I'm sorry, but this is private property," he announced. His tone wasn't threatening, so William tried to be amicable to obtain more information.

"Sorry for the trespass," he contritely replied. "I was admiring the brickwork on this residence." William hesitated for a moment. "I'm a journeyman bricklayer myself."

The foreman looked at him cockeyed as if he didn't know whether to believe him or not and then spoke. "Out of work, it appears, or you wouldn't be wandering about."

The comment took William off guard. Not wanting to sound desperate in that regard, he merely nodded and said, "Between jobs." He paused shortly before asserting himself further. "Forgive me for intruding, but I'm curious who the master brickmaker is or do you work for a builder?"

The foreman didn't answer straightaway. A slight scowl etched his face, and he appeared to study William closer before asking. Obviously he was attempting to figure out if he could be trusted.

"Bradshaw Builders," he eventually responded. "Good company."

"I've heard of them," he countered. "They do more residential than commercial."

"Well, obviously, you're looking for work," the foreman remarked. "Grayson is my name." He offered his hand to shake.

William grabbed it in return. "William Leighton. Pleasure to meet you."

"Leighton," he said, crunching his brows together. "Why do I know that name?"

"Union possibly?" William replied.

"Oh, bloody hell," he spouted. "You're not Hugh Leighton's younger brother are you?"

Instantly William wondered what kind of reputation came to mind at that revelation. No doubt, Hugh had made a name for himself as the union ruffian. "Afraid so."

"I heard about what happened at that warehouse location. You were working for Ashton, right?"

"Yeah, a couple of years. The latest incident put

him out of business as you no doubt caught wind of the affair."

"Well, thank God, we do things on the up-and-up here. All union men. All Manchester-made bricks."

"Good to know," William responded.

"I tell you what," he said, looking at him intently.

William stiffened, hoping it was an offer for work.

"One of my crew here is leaving at the end of the week. The man is moving to London. Poor choice if you ask me," he said, shaking his head. "I could use another hand to finish the job here. There's plenty more work around with new residences going up for the rich businessmen escaping Manchester."

William couldn't believe his luck. "I can get you references," he offered. "Don't know if I can get in touch with Ashton, though, since he may not be too friendly with us union men at the moment."

"Well, listen; I have a decent relationship with George Bradshaw, the owner. He pretty well gives me leave to hire and let go of whomever I damn well please." He paused for a moment and studied William, coming to a decision. "As far as I'm concerned, you're hired, if you want the job. Can you start next week?"

Relief flowed through William's veins like a gush of refreshing water. A huge burden lifted from his shoulders. "Next week you say?"

"It pays thirty-five shillings a week. Right now the crew is working between forty-five and fifty hours a week. Sundays off."

"You've got yourself a new journeyman bricklayer," William said, eagerly offering his handshake again. Luck had fallen into his lap, and he wasn't about to give up a chance for a better income.

"Any idea about housing on this side of town? I'm considering moving."

"Yeah, Lower Broughton has a few areas you might find a room to rent over a shop or a flat," he suggested. "Check with the locals or watch the papers for advertisements."

"Thanks, I'll ask around."

William watched the crew seemingly oblivious to his arrival. Everyone's head was down and focused on the job. The residence would be a grand home when completed. More of his skills could be put to good use instead of working on a warehouse in the middle of the city that looked more like a square box than an architectural wonder. For the first time in weeks, he actually sensed excitement.

"I appreciate the opportunity, Mr. Grayson."

"Bright and early. Seven o'clock on Monday morning."

William's face beamed. He must have found an ounce of favor from the good Lord above to land the job.

Uplifted in spirit, he took his time and walked back to the omnibus station, checking for places to rent along the way. The cleanliness of the locale compared to the nearby slums on Angel Street was far more inviting. He certainly wouldn't miss the neighborhood where he resided, but he would miss worshipping at Saint George's and his mother's grave. Of course, more than the church had captured his interest. Unfortunately, he couldn't do a thing about the circumstances in life that drew him away to better opportunities.

The day slipped by, and William boarded for the

three-mile return to Manchester center. As the horses traveled the road, they would occasionally stop and pick up and drop off riders at various locations. Along the way, William hadn't paid much attention to the passengers coming and going as he sat in the crowded coach. It wasn't until they had finally crossed the Irwell River did he perk up in anticipation of his upcoming stop.

As the horses slowed and a few riders disembarked, others came aboard. He noted out of the corner of his eye that it was a female because of her skirt but didn't pay much attention otherwise. Focused on the busy street outside, he flinched when he heard his name.

"Mr. Leighton, what are you doing here?"

He lifted his head to see Mary, who sat next to him in an empty spot. Suddenly his body was flush next to hers, and a surge of prickly nerves shot through him as if a bolt of lightning had hit him.

"Miss… Miss Booker," he stuttered.

"What a fortuitous surprise finding you here," she exclaimed.

Her excitement about their chance meeting brought the attention of the other passengers as they turned their heads and stared at them. Dumbfounded as to what to say next, he merely looked into her eyes and drowned in a pool of loveliness. The longer he remained quiet, the delight on her face faded. He was acting like a fool and needed to pry his mouth open.

"A chance encounter indeed," he remarked quietly. People had stopped gawking as William lowered his speech.

"Where have you come from?" she asked.

"Broughton," he replied.

"Broughton? Oh my, that is a nice place," she remarked. "My uncle has taken me there for tea at one of the other rectories to meet a friend of his."

"Did you like it?"

"Definitely. Much nicer than crowded and smoky Manchester." She smiled, and excitement returned to her eyes. "In fact, there is a quaint little millinery shop I discovered that just opened in Lower Broughton. I wanted to work there, but uncle forbade it."

"Forbade it?" William scrunched his brows together. "I don't know why he is so insistent that you not be given the opportunity to do something you find pleasurable."

"Marriage and children is all he speaks about for me. In fact, he's been pressuring me to meet certain menfolk in the congregation that I have no interest in whatsoever."

William found his indignation rising, but the timing couldn't be worse. The omnibus came to a halt. He looked into Mary's eyes that pleaded for rescue.

"This is my stop," he said. He grabbed her hand. "Come with me, and let's get a spot of tea somewhere and talk."

Surprised that he actually had the gall to reach out and grab another woman's hand, he tightened his grip, afraid that she would refuse. Instead, she rose to her feet, squeezed his hand in return, and followed him onto the sidewalk. As the horses pulled the bus down the street, William finally let go, suddenly ashamed at his forwardness.

"I'm sorry for clutching your fingers like that, Miss Booker. Do forgive me."

"Nothing to forgive. I'm glad you insisted that we get off together."

"Do you know of anywhere around here we can go?"

"Yes, just around the corner is a nice café. Will that do?"

"Lead the way," he replied.

Had the day been filled with luck, or had every step he'd taken been fate? William couldn't discern which had arrived, but he was anxious to see where it would lead next.

Chapter Ten

TEA FOR TWO

A china teacup. William looked at it awestruck, examining the intricate, flowery pattern. Pubs were more his fare, along with tea at home in a metal mug if he could afford any.

As he sat at the table in the quaint café that Mary had chosen, he looked out of place. His ragged work clothes with his messy hair tucked underneath a worn cap made him appear as a vagrant. A few people showed their displeasure with brooding looks.

Mary didn't seem to mind one bit. Her eyes fixated on him with the same stare he had seen at the vicarage. They spoke volumes, but William wasn't quite sure if he was ready to hear, let alone act on them. On the other hand, one of these days he needed to think about settling down with the right woman. Whatever interest Mary had in him was beyond his comprehension.

"If you think I'm prying, you don't need to answer," she said, starting a conversation. "But what were you doing in Broughton?"

He didn't take the question as nosy. In fact, he had already concluded that she was the type of female he could talk to for hours, confident that she'd care what he had to say.

"I went out of curiosity to look at some potential brickfields," he replied.

"Brickfields?"

William stuck his hand in his vest pocket and retrieved the calling card. He handed it to Mary. "I met this man last week, and he's thinking of starting a brickmaking business. He mentioned the location, so I wanted to see what he was talking about."

She glanced at the card and looked a bit confused, then handed it back to him. "I don't understand a thing about brickfields, brickmaking, or brick setting. It's all very strange to me, but I consider it quite fine that you can line the bricks up in a straight line and make it look nice." Mary chuckled. "You must think me a bit ignorant on the matters of your trade."

"Well, to be fair, I have no idea how you ladies make a hat. All those feathers, ribbons, and whatever else you stick on them to make them fanciful."

He looked at the modest one on her head. Mary appeared self-conscious as she grabbed the ribbon and fiddled with a frayed ending. "You have a fine hat," he assured her so she wouldn't reason he found the excessive wear disagreeable.

"Thank you." Her hands wrapped around her teacup as if she needed the warmth. William didn't know quite what to say in the manner of conversation. After she took a sip of tea, she set it back down on the saucer.

"I heard there was trouble at your work site," Mary mentioned solemnly. "Uncle told me about it the other day. Did you really lose your job?"

Surprised at the declaration, he speculated if the vicar had read it in the newspaper. Then it dawned on him that maybe John realized Mary's interest in him and attempted to dissuade it by noting his unemployed status. William pondered if a man of God could be that sneaky in his dealings. If it was true that he attempted to steer her interest elsewhere, it must be toward employed male folk.

"True, I did lose my job, but I've been offered another." A wide grin filled his face with pride at the day's blessings.

"You did?" She nearly screeched the words, catching the attention of nearby patrons. When she realized what she had done, she brought her hand to her mouth and scrunched her shoulders. "Oh, sorry," she whispered. "I'm prone to excitable outbursts."

William laughed softly. "No need. I was prone to a rather excitable outburst when they offered me work. I'll be in Broughton doing brickwork on residences."

"Oh my." She sighed. "Those grand homes are so lovely."

Her eyes took on a dreamy gaze, and one thought came to mind. "You would make a grand lady in one of those homes," William remarked, imagining her as revered lady in the community.

Regrettably, he would never be able to give her such a place to live. The reality saddened him because she deserved someone better than him with more of a future. Perhaps the vicar was right. He wasn't good enough for her, and the notion burdened him. He might as well be carrying a hod of bricks on his shoulders for the terrible weight of disappointment crushing him at that moment.

"Are you all right?" She creased her brow, noting

his sad thoughts.

"You deserve someone who can give you a splendid home to live in. I'm not that type of gent," he dejectedly announced.

Suddenly her facial expression changed to a stern one that reminded him of his mother about to give him a good scolding when he was five.

"William Leighton," she said with pursed lips. "Don't you ever underestimate what you can accomplish in life. You're a fine man, as far as I'm concerned. I just know in my heart that if you have goals, you'll achieve them if you don't second-guess yourself." She narrowed her eyes. "Besides, it doesn't matter where I live. As long as I'm with the right man, I'll be quite happy, thank you very much." Mary lifted her chin in defiance.

William flinched at her spunky remark, and his surprised facial expression gave way to a smile. Mary's personality, as far as he was concerned, was a treasure indeed. If he ever did make something of himself in life, he wanted a strong woman by his side. Instead of believing he wasn't good enough, something inside William gave him the confidence he could bring her happiness.

Life, though, had given him another direction that would put distance between them. "I'm moving," he soberly remarked.

"Moving?" Mary cocked her head. The twinkle in her eye dimmed.

"I had thought of moving to Broughton, but I've yet to find a place. Makes sense to be closer to my work."

Her breath hitched in her throat as if she were

choking on his words. "Will I not see you again? Will you not worship at Saint George's any longer?"

"Do you want to see me again?" It was a foolish question because he could tell from the longing in her eyes that she did.

"How can I tell you what I want, Mr. Leighton, without sounding like a terribly loose woman with no morals? My uncle would thrash me if he knew I had spoken such intimate thoughts." She pulled her eyes away in embarrassment.

Surprised at her fear of the vicar, William leaned hard into the chair. For a moment he wished Hugh would give him advice on how to pursue a female. After all, he and Aaron had married good matches, and both had born children aplenty. They were settled in life while he languished, afraid to express his interest as a man should.

Struggling like a coward, he wanted her to say it first. Then, if he did, would the vicar disapprove of his intention to court his niece? Apparently, in John's eyes, William's status in life wasn't good enough for Mary. Her uncle had plans and other gents in mind. Obstacles loomed everywhere, and if he wanted his blessing, he would have to succeed financially.

When he saw her hand nervously clutch the napkin on the table, he reached across and took it in his. Her fingers were like the frosty winter's morning.

"I don't want your uncle to thrash you, so I'll say the words for us both." A lump formed in this throat, and William gave it a good swallow. The tips of his fingers trembled with nerves as he continued to touch her flesh. "Now I could be wrong, but I think you might like me a bit," he shyly announced, lowering his gaze.

"You can tell me if I'm wrong, and I won't be offended by the truth now." He looked at Mary, and her eyes had widened in anticipation, giving him the courage to continue. "I'll admit I've taken a liking to you too."

"You have?" She squeezed his hand in return, and the brightness in her eyes returned.

"Yes, but maybe we ought not to tell your uncle. Do you mind keeping it a secret for now?"

"No, I don't. I'd feel better if he didn't know."

Her emphatic answer gave William hope, and he pondered for a second, then spoke. "I wouldn't call it lying like a sin—just not telling him until we see how the courting goes."

"You want to court me?" she squeaked.

He nodded his head affirmatively. "I'm ignorant when it comes to courting a woman, mind you. But I guess I can figure it out."

Mary let out a soft chuckle. "I'm sure you'll do just fine."

"Don't know how much time I'll have except for Sundays. With work and all it will be hard." William's enthusiasm faded.

"I understand," Mary replied. "We'll just take good care of the time we have."

"Of course, how are you going to get away from your uncle? You'll be with a man unchaperoned. Don't want to ruin your reputation."

"Well, I have an idea that we can meet at my friend's home. I'm sure she wouldn't mind letting us use her parlor or let us walk in her garden. She knew my parents when they were alive."

The arrangement sounded plausible, so William agreed. "Sounds fine to me."

Mary glanced at the clock on the wall and became agitated. "I need to get back to the vicarage," she said. "Uncle will wonder why I'm delayed."

"Shall I walk you back? I don't like the idea of you going alone past Angel Meadows."

"I would be most appreciative," she replied.

William paid for their tea and walked outdoors with Mary by his side. He felt out of sorts and wondered if he should offer his arm to her as the wealthy gents did with their women. He hesitated for so long that by the time they had reached the vicarage by Oldham Road, they had arrived.

They stopped a few yards away and faced each other. "I'll come to church this Sunday," he announced.

"Good. I'll arrange it with Miss Beecham that we can meet afterward at her home. It's not far from church."

"Will she mind?"

"No, I don't believe so. She's a good friend and knows that I don't like Uncle pressuring me to do as he pleases."

William didn't know what to do next. The idea of kissing her hand or giving her an embrace was out of the question. As far as smooching a woman, he hadn't the slightest idea what it would feel like. Her lips looked full and ripe as a peach and undoubtedly tasted sweet.

"Well, I'll be going," he said, "Miss Booker." He tipped his hat.

"Call me Mary, please." Her cheeks blushed. "May I call you William?"

"Call me Will, if you'd like. I'm sure I'll enjoy the

way my name sounds when you say it," he replied. "I mostly hear William shouted by men or my brother."

"I'd prefer addressing you as William in a soft tone so you enjoy the sound."

Suddenly he couldn't breathe another word from between his lips. His heart started to race, and it frightened the daylights out of him.

"See you… see you Sunday, Mary," he said. A terrible urge to kiss her on the cheek made him take a step forward. When he did, her eyes widened as if she expected him to do something, but they were standing on the walkway near the street. People and carriages were passing by, and he wasn't ready—especially for a public display of affection.

"Good day."

He tipped his hat and briskly walked down the sidewalk, afraid to turn around and look at the expression on her face. With a bit of luck, she understood his awkward, abrupt departure. Courting a lady was something he knew absolutely nothing about, and it wasn't going to be easy.

Chapter Eleven

BRAINS OR BRAWN

Hugh, Jackson, and Bailey sat at the Crown & Cushion, having an ale while plotting their next move. The union had sanctioned retaliation against another brickmaker, and they had a ten-pound incentive to split five ways. The target was a new brickmaking mechanism at Sheffield's Brickmaking Company. The owner had set up shop and hired nonunion men to run the contraption.

"There's a night watchman on the grounds," Bailey commented. "Hugh, you'll need to bring the pistol to take care of it if he gives us trouble."

Jackson offered a note of reason. "Let's just knock him out with a brick and tie him up. No need to add murder to the list."

Hugh laughed. "Someone is always suggesting murder. I'll kill any damn dog that comes at me but am careful not to have human blood on me hands unless he shoots first."

They all grunted in unison as if they agreed to his comment. "Jackson, you bringing the naphtha?"

"Yeah, two bottles should do it. We have a few other lads lined up coming with sticks just in case we need more force."

"It's decided then. We're burning the building

with the machine?" Hugh asked.

"That's the plan. Should be a nice night for a bonfire." Bailey chortled.

After gulping the ale in his glass, Hugh set it down on the table. "All right, lads. Two this morning, let's meet at the place we talked about. Make sure we avoid any constables walking their routes."

The three shook hands as they always did for luck before an attack. Hugh's earnings from his night outings were adding up to a nice little savings he planned to use to get out of the slum neighborhood. He slapped his cap back on his head, shoved his hands in his pocket, and exited the pub. The night air chilled him a bit, and he wondered how William had fared looking for work.

The money he had given him had come out of his pocket. He lied that the union had provided compensation for those who lost the job. Since he had been one of the perpetrators that night, wielding a sledgehammer against the wall that William had worked on, it was the least he could do. If the damn contractors and masters would just keep the rules, he wouldn't have to be part of the violence. All the same, he would continue to enforce the union guidelines come hell or high water.

Work for him had been sporadic in the past year. He seemed to spend more time embroiled in the union matters than with a trowel in his hand, slapping mortar on top of bricks. The latest job had ended, and the master bricklayer he had been working for just picked up another contract on the other side of town. The days would be lengthy as well as the nights, acting as the devil imparting retribution.

As he turned the corner to walk down the street to his residence, a prostitute came out from the dark shadows and stood before him.

"A few shillings, dearie, and I can give ye a good time down the alley," she said enticingly. She opened the shawl wrapped around her shoulders and flashed him her exposed breasts. They were plump as a melon, and he stared at them in disbelief. Her nipples were dark like honey and hard.

"Nice tits," he slurred. "Wouldn't mind a suck, but I'm not buying tonight," he reiterated. Truth be told, he rarely partook in the street trash until his wife got pregnant. She didn't want a thing to do with him, and like any other man, he needed a release. Thank God, he hadn't caught the street disease from the prostitute he used. She was a young thing and new to the trade. The older harlots, like the one who stood in front of him, probably would give him more than he paid for in the way of fleshly delights.

Eliza was a good woman, but she was nothing to speak of when they joined in bed. There wasn't an ounce of passion in her bones, and he could tell she hated physical relations. She merely tolerated him by spreading her legs and lying there as dormant as the pillow. Perhaps it was best because they wouldn't be saddled with eight children as Aaron had, breeding one after another. By the time Aaron's wife couldn't bear any more, he would doubtless have a few more youngsters.

"You sure?" She pushed her bosom together for a tease.

"Aye, I'm sure," he said, shaking his head. "Cover yourself up. It's getting cold outside."

She reached out, grabbed his forearm, and dug her nails into his coat sleeve in desperation. "I'm good at other things too," she offered, grabbing his crotch with her other hand. "Like those Frenchie whores."

The woman wouldn't give up, and she irritated the hell out of him. He put both hands on her shoulders and gave her a slight shove. "I said not tonight."

Hugh pushed past her and continued down the street. The usual drunks staggered out of pubs, and more prostitutes gave him the eye as he walked by. The neighborhood was a hellhole, and though they didn't live in the thick of Angel Meadows, he and William weren't far from the locality they both wanted to escape.

Finally he approached his residence and went indoors. Eliza was sitting by the fireplace with their babe in her lap, feeding her from her swollen milk-filled breast. He chuckled at the notion that men suckled throughout their life on a woman's bust one way or another. Nipples were a strange thing that drew babies and men alike.

"Home," he announced as if she didn't seem to notice that he entered the room. "Anything for dinner?" He glanced around and saw a pot of stew. "Never mind. I see the fixin's," he said. Hugh grabbed a wooden bowl, spooned a hearty portion into the center, and sat down at the table. A loaf of bread sat on a plate, and he ripped the end off and dipped it in the juicy mix of meat and potatoes. After taking a taste, he moaned at the flavor.

"Damn, woman, you're a good cook when I can get us a piece of decent meat." He filled his mouth with the tender morsel and savored each bite. Eliza, however, remained strangely quiet. The babe finished, and his wife stuffed her breast back into the bodice of her dress. Hugh decided to give her a few shillings to buy a new frock. Her clothes were beginning to look drab and old.

Eliza took Margaret and laid her down in the cradle that he had made. They couldn't afford to buy a decent one with the fancy frills, but he was a darn good craftsman with wood too if he put his mind to it. After covering up the baby, she came over and sat down at the table with him. Her face remained grim, and Hugh knew she had a bone to pick.

"Are you going out tonight at some ungodly hour?"

"Yep," he said, not giving a care to her discontent about the outing. "We got work to do."

"Work," she snarled. "I would hardly call what you and your thugs do as work."

Hugh sighed and put down his spoon on the table. All he wanted was a quiet dinner. By the sneer on his wife's lips, they were on the brink of another spat.

"What I do, Eliza, is necessary for everyone in the union. If someone doesn't keep the rules, there's a price to pay. That's all there is to it." He picked up his utensil, dipped it in the bowl, and loaded it with another mouthful. "If you don't mind, I'm hungry," he announced, talking with a mouthful. "Got a long night ahead of me."

"One of these days, you're going to get shot or arrested, Hugh. Then who will take care of the baby and me?" Her voice pitched at him.

"God, woman, you worry about everything.

Nothing is going to happen to me, and it brings extra money into the household."

"I don't care about the money." She crossed her arms like a child having a tantrum.

Hugh expelled a scoffing laugh. "You don't care? Then you're a fool." He slammed his spoon down on the tabletop. "Takes money to live with a roof over your head." He nodded at the ceiling above. "Takes money to put food in your belly so your tits grow big and you can feed the little one. Living takes money, Eliza." He huffed in ire. "You want to end up in the workhouse? Is that what you want?"

After screeching his question at his wife, she flinched at his bellowing voice. His nostrils pulled back, making him look like a bear. Fed up, he pushed back from the table, got up, and walked to the mantel to grab the bottle of whiskey that sat on top. After taking off the cap, he took a swig and let the alcohol burn down his throat.

"Sorry," she sheepishly said in a trembling voice. "Didn't mean to upset you."

He barely heard the words, and for the life of him, he had nothing to say in response. After gulping another swig, he had decided he didn't want to stay in the same room with her until the job tonight. Hugh headed for the cupboard and reached on top to retrieve his pistol that was wrapped in an old rag and out of Eliza's reach. He grabbed it, wiped it off, and then shoved it in his waistband, hidden by his shirt and overcoat. Eliza watched him, and her anger contorted her face.

"Must you?" she asked in a pleading tone. "I hate that thing."

"You keep to the house and take care of the baby," he ordered in a dark tone, pointing his finger at her. "What I do is none of your concern." His feet stomped across the wood plank floor that creaked with the weight of his body. After grabbing the doorknob, he called over his shoulder at her. "I'll be back in the morning after the job's done." He slammed the door shut and headed for the nearest pub to drown his irritation in the liquid bliss of alcohol.

The six men with hats pulled down low and collars pulled up high congregated in the alley a block away from Sheffield's brickmaking business. A cold and unwelcomed drizzle fell, and the thick, foggy night air gave them cover in the darkness. Bailey returned after inspecting the location before the rest of the men proceeded.

"There's a tiny shed with a watchman at the gate entrance. The entire area is fenced off like a fortress." He sighed in disappointment. "This is going to be a hard break."

"Any dogs?" Hugh asked, thinking about the last one he shot.

"Didn't see any."

Jackson came up with a stupid idea. "Why don't we just rush the guardhouse, knock out the guard, and be done with it?"

"Don't like it," Hugh said. "The gate's on a busy street. A constable will see us for sure if they've upped patrols in the area." He considered the situation for a moment. "I say we just break through the fence from the back alley and sneak our way into the compound.

Once we set the building on fire, the guard will surely leave his post and we can escape the way we came in."

Bailey moaned. "I hate fences. Don't forget I have bottles of naphtha in me sack. Don't wanna blow up before we get to the main building."

The other three held bludgeons in their hands ready to wield at whomever they could, but their eyes were wide with fear. They were newcomers to the enforcement outings, but they'd soon learn.

"Follow me," Hugh sternly instructed.

They filed one by one behind him, darting in and out of the shadows until they reached the far parameter of the fence line. After finding a portion of the fence where he could easily pull off rotten boards, they opened an area large enough for all of them to squeeze in and out of the yard.

Single file, they crouched down through the opening and made their way in the dark. The main building, which they assumed housed the brickmaking machine, stood about sixty yards from the guardhouse. Hugh approached a window and peered inside but couldn't see a thing.

"I say we just light the bottles and throw 'em inside. They'll explode and start the fire well enough. What do you think?" Hugh asked. In the distance, a dog barked.

Jackson's eyes widened like saucers. "I say we better do something quick because here comes that damn guard, waving a gun in the air."

"Who's there?" a deep voice bellowed in their direction, running toward them. "Who's there?"

"It's now or never, Bailey," Hugh snarled. "Light one and give it to me. I'll toss it through the window.

You do the other."

Bailey nervously struck a match and lit the fuses at the end of the old bottle. The illumination burst through the darkness, revealing all five of them, standing there with sticks in hand, and firebombs.

"Halt!" the guard screeched.

A gunshot rang out, and the ball whizzed by his ear. He flung the bottle at the window, it broke, and the contents exploded into a ball of flames. The firelight revealed the strange contraption inside. Bailey threw his bottle, which added to the explosion that nearly knocked them off their feet.

"Run, boys!" Hugh bellowed at the top of his lungs. They turned heel and headed to the fence. A few more shots rang out. Instinctively, Hugh pulled out his pistol from his waistband, swung around, aimed it toward the guard, and pulled the trigger. He wasn't the best of shot, but this one hit the man's upper right thigh with a thud.

"Holy shite!" Jackson yelled. He grabbed Hugh's jacket and tugged on it. "Get out of here, man, before the police get here."

Shaking uncontrollably about what he did, Hugh clutched the gun and fled with the remainder of the lads. He had never shot anybody before. The gun felt like hellfire in his hands. The flames from the explosion shot straight up into the air, lighting up the neighborhood like the noonday.

The plan had been for each to disburse, which three of them had done, running in different directions down alleyways or side streets. Bailey and Hugh remained together, but as they rounded the corner of the next block, they came face-to-face with a constable running toward the fire. Rather than panicking, Hugh stumbled like a drunk and bellowed out an old tavern song.

"A thousand times he kiss'd her, laying her on the green. But as he farther press'd her, her pretty leg was seen..."

Bailey speedily caught on to his trickery and swayed too, joining in with the ruse.

"Where you men coming from?" the constable barked, halting them in their step. He grabbed his club and held it in his hand, ready to swing it at any moment.

"The bed of prostitutes and the ale of the pub," Hugh slurred.

Bailey threw his arm around Hugh's shoulder. "Just trying to get me mate home so his wife don't give him a good whoopin' for being out all night," he said, grinning like a mischievous fool.

The policeman took note of the flames shooting upward, and his eyes widened in urgency. "Get the hell home," he yelled. "I've got better things to do than lock you up for being drunk and disorderly." Without another word, he ran toward Sheffield's property.

"You heard the man," Hugh yelped. "Let's get home." With that, they quickened their step and disappeared into the night. Tomorrow Hugh would pay the boys their due for a job well done.

Chapter Twelve

The Aftermath of Terror

The following morning, Margaret wailed for a feeding, which woke Hugh up out of a deep sleep. Disoriented and still exhausted, he rolled over to see Eliza get up from bed and tend to their daughter. He pulled the blanket to his shoulder and swung to his side. Instead of sleep returning to give him rest, the incident that occurred five hours earlier haunted him.

When he closed his eyes, he saw the flames of hell and heard the whizzing bullet fly by his head. The click of the trigger and hearing the bullet lodge in the watchman's leg sounded sickening. He must have hit bone to cause the thud rather than traveling through soft flesh. When it hit, the man fell to the ground, grabbing his leg and hollering in agony. Hugh shuddered at what he had done but remained thankful he hadn't killed the unfortunate bloke. The idea of being caught and hanging by the neck until dead would deter him in the future from aiming for the chest.

Hugh rolled on his side and watched Eliza. He hoped to get her pregnant again because he wanted a son. Every man wants sons to carry on their name and legacy. At one time he thought he had the perfect lad to do just that, but heaven had other ideas.

"What kind of God takes children all the time?" he grumbled under his breath. Not the kind he cared to worship by any means.

"Did you say something?" Eliza swung around and stared at him.

"No," he answered, not in any mood to discuss the matter.

"Did everything go all right last night with work?"

Hugh shot up and sat on the edge of the bed, driving his fingers through his unruly hair. "Yeah, fine," he muttered, standing to his feet.

He poured water into the washbasin from the pitcher, then splashed his face a few times. The cooling liquid helped clear his mind. After he patted his face with a towel, he grabbed his trousers from the floor.

"Any clean shirts around?" He glanced at the few clothes they stuffed in an old, unsteady bureau absent a wooden leg.

"Aye, I washed two days ago," Eliza responded.

He pulled out the drawer and found the shirt. "I need to get to work soon," he announced. "New job coming up, and the foreman is giving us the drawings to look at."

Margaret ceased sucking on his wife's breast, and she put her back in the cradle. When Hugh saw her exposed bosom, he came up from behind her and clasped his fingers around her flesh. "Our daughter's not the only one that needs comfort," he said, squeezing her lightly. Eliza's soft and subtle flesh aroused him.

"I got a few minutes." He groaned. Hugh's hand

fiddled with her nightgown and clawed at it until the hem was in his hand. Naked and fresh for the taking, he pulled Eliza to the bed and gave her a playful shove down on the mattress. "I'm hungry too." He flashed a lustful glare and covered her mouth and kissed her ardently. Like a dead fish floating on the water top, she lay beneath him unresponsive. Fed up with her defiance, he pulled away.

"Can't you even put your goddamn arms around me and give me a hug? I'm your husband, and I need you." She stared at him blankly. "Besides, I want another child."

Eliza turned her head to the side. "You know how I feel about it," she responded in a cold tone of indifference.

Without any affectionate foreplay, Hugh shoved himself inside her body and took what he wanted. She gasped at the onslaught. Nothing ever changed with Eliza. She lay there beneath him as he thrust into her body and released himself with a deep groan. The loathing she held about the act oozed from every pore of her stiff figure. Rolling off her, he flopped onto the mattress in frustration.

"There's not an ounce of affection I receive from you, Eliza, in bed or out. Obviously, your love for me has died." He sat up, swung his legs over the side of the bed, and looked at her.

"I despise the physical act," she retorted with a firm tone. "I've told you so repeatedly."

"You might enjoy it if you would relax and let me pleasure you."

She snarled at him. "How can a woman relax? If it weren't for the fact that this imposition is the only way for me to get pregnant, I'd never let you touch me again."

"How kind you are," he snapped. "And to think last night I turned down a prostitute wanting to suck me…"

"Don't tell me!" Eliza put her hands on her ears. "I hate you when you speak of such filthy things."

Hugh's heart weighed heavily. He had borne the burden of her disinterest for years. Ever since their firstborn died, her desire for intimacy died as well. Margaret's birth was a miracle of conception. Regardless, he wanted more children.

"Well, you better come to terms with the fact, Eliza, that I want a son. Since nature has decided this is how it's done, I'm not going to stop poking you with me cock until your belly is full with another child."

Fuming, he slipped on his pants, grabbed his shirt, and stomped out of the room. "Damn women," he spat. William showed wisdom in waiting for a wife. He had spared himself years of emotional turmoil from the female sex who made no sense whatsoever.

He had just arrived downstairs when he heard a knock at the door. Wondering who it could be so early in the morning, he cautiously peeked out the window to see Bailey standing on the other side. After opening it, he glowered.

"What are you doing here?"

Bailey glanced to his right, left, and then entered. "Wanted to make sure I'm not being followed," he said.

Nervous, Hugh shut the door. "What's going on?"

"I had one of the lads walk by Sheffield's this morning. The building burned to the ground for sure, and there's a black, mangled piece of machinery in it."

"Good," Hugh spouted in relief. "The owner got what he had coming to him." He thought of the guard. "Any word on…"

"I don't know what happened to him," Bailey replied. "Nothing bad, I would think, since you just shot him in the leg."

"What?" Eliza screeched at the top of her lungs. Hugh swung around to see her standing by the staircase. "What the hell did you do, Hugh Leighton?" The ire in her eyes gave Bailey a shock.

"You best be going. I'll talk to you later," he said. Bailey didn't hesitate to exit the residence a second later, leaving Hugh to deal with his wife.

"It's nothing that concerns you, Eliza. I've told you repeatedly the union matters are me business."

"Where's the gun?" she ranted, running past him to the cupboard. Her hands reached on top, trying to feel for the pistol.

"It's not there," Hugh calmly remarked. "I've hid it elsewhere."

"Did you shoot the watchman?" Eliza grabbed him by the shoulder in desperation. She wanted an answer, so he gave it to her.

"Aye, I shot the watchman in the leg," he roared. "Now that's the end of it."

Never in a million years did he expect his wife to act in such a manner, but she lifted her right hand and slapped him hard across his cheek. When she tried to give him another wallop, he grabbed her wrist and prevented the hit.

"Stop it now," he barked, twisting her joint until she yelped.

"You're going to be the death of me," she cried. "Let me go!"

Hugh released her, and she backed away from him and eyed him up and down in disgust. "Wait until William hears of it," she warned with pursed lips. "He'll give you hell for what you've done."

"William doesn't need to know of it," Hugh barked. He took an angry step, closing the distance between them. "You keep your mouth shut, woman," he warned, shaking his bony finger in her face. "You hear me? I'll have none of it—you meddling in me affairs with me brother."

His wife didn't speak, but he could tell by the look in her eye she planned to use it against him one day. He wanted to slap her around the house to put some sense into her head. Every man possessed the right in the eyes of the law to give his wife moderate physical correction as he saw fit, and this was the time she needed it.

Eliza backed away from him. The rage in his eyes told her what would come next. He grabbed her by the shoulders, dug his fingers into her flesh, and shook her hard.

"You keep your mouth shut." He smacked her hard across the face in return for the one she had given him. Her flesh reddened at the blow. "I won't say this again; this is none of your business. Tend to our home and our child—that's all you're here to do."

Eliza's eyes widened, and just then, Margaret let out a high-pitch wail. He dropped his hands and stepped back.

"Go," he yelled. "Take care of our daughter."

Eliza spun around and ran upstairs with tears

streaming down her cheeks. Hugh didn't like being rough with her. It usually only happened when he drank too much and she irritated him about something trivial. A push there, a shove here, a slap to shut her up. Nevertheless, too much was at stake for her to go mouthing off what happened last night. He would deal with that bit of knowledge when the time was right. Now he was still too raw about what he had done.

Hugh slipped on his shoes, grabbed his cap and coat, and headed out the door. He slammed it to make his last point to Eliza upstairs. As he stomped down the street toward work, his mind swirled like a hornet's nest. Between the lack of sleep, his meddling wife, and last night's outrage, he was ready to scream bloody murder at anybody that came near him. With a bit of luck, by the time he spoke with his foreman about the new job, his boiling blood would calm to a slow simmer.

William would know about last night by reading it in the newspaper in the next day. Usually when he did read about the union's latest violence, he pressed Hugh about his involvement. He wouldn't find out from him, and Hugh would make sure that Jackson, Bailey, and the other boys kept their mouths shut as well. When he paid them their share later today, he would tell them to keep his involvement in the shooting to themselves.

Chapter Thirteen

THE ART OF COURTING

William wore his best clothes, which were shabby in appearance. He swore one day he would rid himself of what he owned and purchase a fine used frock coat and vest that showed little wear. The day before, he paid for a bath at the washhouse and then found a barber for a haircut that he desperately needed.

As he sat in the pew of Saint George's, listening to the vicar say the partings words of "Go in peace," he pondered what lay ahead. Today he would spend a good amount of time with Mary, which both terrified and excited him.

Finally the service ended. The congregation rose to their feet and filed down the aisle to the exit to give the vicar a word of greeting or a handshake. William waited for Mary to approach. In her hand, she clutched a small note.

"Good morning." She greeted him as if it were a friendly churchgoing hello but then slipped the paper in his hand. "Here's the address. Meet you there shortly," she whispered and then scurried out the door.

He left the pew and stepped into the aisle way to the church foyer. William halted behind another couple and eventually followed them out so that the vicar wouldn't suspect anything out of the ordinary. When he reached the large wooden door, he spoke to John.

"I've come to say that I will be leaving Saint George's parish as I'm moving to Broughton."

An unexpected flash of disappointment etched his face. "I'm sad to hear of it, William. Might I ask why?"

"Work," he answered. "I have a new opportunity, building residences there."

"Oh, I see. Well, I have a colleague there at Saint John's on Wellington Street, who is a fine gentleman. I'll send him a note to watch for your arrival soon."

"I'd appreciate that," William said, offering a handshake. "Thank you, by the way, for burying mother. I won't be a stranger to her grave for visits as I'm sure Hugh will come periodically as well."

"That's good to know," he replied.

A gentleman behind him cleared his throat as if he wanted William to cease the chitchat and move along. Without hesitating, he did and walked down the pathway to the road. He halted for a moment, looked at the note that Mary gave him, and read the address off Oldham Road. It wasn't too far away from Saint George's, so William decided to walk to provide Mary ample time to arrive ahead of him.

Each step that he took added to the nervous jitters in his body. He started to sweat, so he took off his frock coat and walked in his high-cut collared vest and white shirt. His frayed cuffs ruined everything, but he couldn't afford a new shirt. Like it or not, this was his lot in life, and until things improved, food in his belly and a roof over his head would be a priority.

Finally, after a leisurely stroll, he arrived at the location. It was a decent terrace cottage with delicate lace curtains on the windows. The door was painted bright red with a gold-colored door handle and knocker. As he was about to walk up to the stoop, the curtains parted, and he caught sight of Mary peeking at him. She flashed a welcoming smile, which calmed his jitters. The curtain dropped back in place, and before he could knock, the door flung open.

"Hello, William." Mary's sweet voice sounded musical in his ears, and her eyes were bright with excitement.

"Hello."

"Yes, hello."

Another woman pushed next to Mary and examined him with interest. She appeared to be in her midforties. A bright blue dress with a white lace collar fitted tightly on her slim frame.

"I'm Miriam Beecham, and I've been told by this young lady that you wish to use my parlor to conduct polite conversation." She eyed him playfully. "Is that true, Mr. Leighton?"

Mary giggled. "Miriam, stop teasing him." She pushed her aside with her hip.

William chortled a laugh. "Yes, Miss Beecham. That is my intent. May I come in?"

"Hmm," she mused, eyeing up and down again. "What do you think, Mary? Shall we let this stranger enter my home? I have no dog to attack him if he gets aggressive."

"He's a perfect gentleman, Miriam." Mary opened the door wider. "Come in, William, and pay no attention to her. She's a clown."

William removed his hat and stepped indoors. Mary closed it behind him while Miriam directed his steps.

"This way to the parlor," she said. "I have a few questions to ask you before I allow this mischief between the two of you to continue."

Miriam's finger pointed at an empty settee, so William complied. To his surprise, Mary flopped on the seat next to him in an excitable movement that caught him off guard. Miriam, on the other hand, stood in front of them, peering down like a general in the guards.

"Now, my friend here tells me you wish to court her. Is that true?"

William wasn't sure how much authority the lady had over Mary's life or who she was for that matter. Instead of answering, he pried into their association. "I'm curious what your relationship is with Mary before divulging my intentions."

"Ooh, he has nerve, I see," Miriam said, turning toward Mary.

"Shall I answer?" Mary asked.

Miriam shook her head. "No, dear, let me since the question was pointedly asked in my direction." The lady looked at William and calmly spoke with her hands clasped before her waist. "I was Mary's governess for many years, so you see I have an interest in her welfare."

Governess. William sucked in a surprised breath. If her parents were wealthy enough to provide her a governess, that's possibly why she had learned to read and write as well. He knew nothing about her background but struggled with unworthiness if she had come from a middle-class family. His curiosity about her parent's demise came to the forefront. Rather than ask such a personal question at that time, he decided it best to broach that subject in private.

"Understandable that you have her welfare in mind," William responded. "Then I can assure you that my intentions toward Mary are honorable and that as a man of integrity I shall treat her with the utmost respect she deserves." The words sounded grandiose compared to his lowly occupation of slathering mortar on top of a brick, but for some reason he wanted to act as if he had more to offer Mary than borderline poverty.

"Sounds good enough for me," Miriam said. "I'll be back with the tea."

Miriam scurried from the room, and William couldn't help but grin about what happened.

"Don't take her too seriously," Mary remarked. "She has been so gracious to allow me to use her parlor so we can talk away from Uncle."

"Does she consider your uncle too strict in his dealings with you?"

"Oh, she's not fond of him, I can say that for certain. She has told him so to his face when he insisted on taking me into his home when father died."

"Mary, I hope you don't mind, but may I inquire as to what happened to your parents?"

"Yes, of course," she said in a low tone. Her eyes took on a dark shade of sadness. "My mother passed away nearly five years ago. She had a late pregnancy in life but was unable to birth the child without complications. Something went terribly wrong, and she died, along with the baby."

"Oh, I'm so sorry," William replied.

"Father, I'm afraid, had a broken heart for years and blamed himself. He never really got over her death. His health deteriorated after we buried her. The surgeon said his heart failed, and six months ago he passed away."

"Do you have any siblings?"

"Yes, a brother, but he lives in Edinburgh. He loves it up north, so he took his inheritance, wife, and children, and moved there from Birmingham."

"He didn't take you?"

"I didn't want to go, frankly. We aren't that close, William, as he is much older than I am."

Mary fell silent for a few moments as William pondered their common situations with siblings. Miriam returned with a tray of refreshments and set them down on a side table.

"Now I'll leave the two of you alone because I trust you both explicitly." She glanced approvingly at Mary and closed the double door to the parlor.

"Miriam is such a dear. She wanted me to come live with her after father died. Uncle, however, insisted since he was my closest relative and that I should stay with him instead."

"It seems your uncle has a strong hand in your life." William reined in his irritation because a few swear words danced at the tip of his tongue.

Mary rose and poured each of them a cup of tea. She handed a cup and saucer to William, which he took in hand. He couldn't quite get used to fancy teacups for some odd reason. After Mary sat back down, he pondered about what to talk about next since idle conversation with a woman proved challenging. Mary appeared as ill at ease as he did when she silently sipped her tea and stared off in the direction of a potted plant in the corner.

"Have... have you thought any more about work at that millinery shop in Broughton?" He wasn't sure if the question would make her sad, but at least it was a conversational topic.

"Oh, yes, I think about it all the time. Miriam wants me to defy Uncle. She said if he kicks me out of the vicarage, I can come and live here."

"I would never kick anyone out of my home because of something as trivial." A wicked idea teased his brain. "If you did find a job there, you might be able to get a room at a nice boarding house in Lower Broughton."

"Could I afford one as a sales clerk?" she asked.

William shrugged his shoulders. "Don't know, but you should find out."

"I suppose," she mused. The twinkle in her eye returned.

"We would be closer to one another—both of us living in the same area, then we could spend more time together." Suggesting the notion sounded logical to William.

Mary's spine straightened like an arrow, and she pulled back her shoulders. He couldn't tell if the thought frightened her or enthralled her by the expression on her face. Her facial expression brightened.

"Oh, that would be wonderful, William."

"I dare say it would be. We could be friends being

in a new part of town. If you ever needed anything, I'd make sure to help you in any way needed." As soon as the word *friends* left his lips, Mary's smile contorted into a grimace.

"Friends, Mr. Leighton? Is that how you see me—a potential lady friend?" Mary set her cup down on the table, acting slightly irritated about his remark. She tilted her head at him.

"Well, I—"

"Let me be very clear," she announced, cutting off his words. "I have no desire to be your lady friend. I have designs on you, Mr. Leighton, and I'm the type of woman who gets what I want."

William's jaw dropped at least an inch, and his heart rate increased to a thump in his throat. The woman was undoubtedly brash, to say the least, with a mind of her own. Besides having pleasing physical attributes, her personality was unlike any other female he had the acquaintance to meet. God, he loved every inch of her, and the fire of desire burned in the core of his soul.

"I like you, Mary," he firmly declared. William reached over and grabbed her hand. "You are one fine woman—attractive, spunky, humorous, and downright adorable." Her cheeks blushed profusely. "I don't know how long this courting business needs to take place, but if I were a betting man, I'd say it's going to be a short one."

"Oh, William, I so admire you," she babbled. "You have a kind heart and ambition. I like that in a man." She giggled like a schoolgirl. "I'm sure you realize my regard for you by now."

Miriam must have been listening at the door

because suddenly it swung open and she stood in the threshold with her hands on her hips. "All right, enough of that gushing foolery going on. Before you know it, the two of you will be kissing, and I won't have it in my house behind closed doors."

William grinned because he wanted to kiss Mary before Miriam barged into the room.

"So are we done for the day?" Miriam asked.

Mary looked disappointed but agreed she needed to get back to the vicarage. "Yes, I think so as I told Uncle I would only be an hour."

"Mary, I think that William here has a brilliant idea. Go get that job you want and find a place of your own. You're a young lady old enough to make your own decisions. Your father would want that for you instead of being under your uncle's thumb. As brothers-in-law, they never did see eye to eye, and I'm certain your father wouldn't agree to how he's keeping you now."

"I wholeheartedly agree," William replied.

"You're probably right." Mary sighed. "Maybe I'll try for the position."

"Good!" Miriam responded. "Now, sir, best you get going. I don't want her uncle seeing the two of you together. He's liable to lock her in the church bell tower if he does."

William reluctantly rose to his feet, and Mary did as well.

"I'll walk you to the door," she announced.

When they reached the threshold, William turned and gazed at Mary, pleased with how well their time together went. "I'll keep in touch and let you know when I find a new place myself."

"All right, and I'll do the same." William put his hat back on.

"Well, goodbye then."

When his eyes considered her pink cheek, he recognized what needed to happen. William gave her a quick peck and then ran out the door and onto the street. When he turned around to wave goodbye, Mary's hand was on her face where his lips had touched. She was such a sweetheart. The remainder of the day he would be miserable without her at his side.

Chapter Fourteen

THE SIBLING GAP

William focused on finding a place to live in Broughton to such an extent that he hadn't read the news for over a week. After searching for days, he finally discovered a small but convenient location in Lower Broughton where he rented a basement flat underneath a terrace house. He moved what little belongings he possessed and paid a carter to take them to the address.

With all the excitement of a new residence and Mary on his mind, he hadn't given much of anything second thought. As agreed, he arrived at his new job on Monday ready to work on the house that he had seen the week before, eager to put his skills to better use.

Grayson greeted him as he approached but didn't look too eager to see his arrival. With the dark look in his eyes, it made William wonder if he had changed his mind.

"Before I let you on the job," he began in a deep tone, "Bradshaw wants to know if you had anything to do with the attack at Sheffield's." The foreman crossed his arms as if he were ready to prevent him from taking a step farther.

William scrunched his brows together in

confusion, having no idea what the man was talking about. "What attack?"

"The one that happened last week," he said, clearly irritated at William's response. "Where the hell you been, Leighton?"

William took off his cap and held it in his hand. He scratched the side of his head as his scalp tingled from dread. "I've been busy, finding a place to live and moving," he shakily responded. "What the hell happened at Sheffield's?"

"I suppose this means you haven't spoken to your brother in the past few days either." Grayson pulled his mouth to one side.

"No, I haven't." The confusion about the conversation cleared. All Grayson had to do was speak Hugh's name, and the fog burned away, leaving an obvious reason for Bradshaw's concern.

"My brother and I are not that close," William responded, putting distance between them. "He doesn't confide in me regarding his whereabouts because he knows I disagree with his affairs."

Grayson dropped his arms from his waist and relaxed his stance. "Apparently a group of union thugs attacked Sheffield's and destroyed the brickmaking machine. They firebombed the building, and one of them brought a pistol."

"Oh, dear God," William groaned, knowing that implicated Hugh. "Did anyone get hurt?"

"The guard was shot in the leg. He'll live, but the incident has all the builders and master bricklayers on edge."

"No doubt," William replied with pursed lips. His deep-seated anger about Hugh boiled in his gut, and his lip twitched, wanting to let out a flurry of curses.

"I told Bradshaw I hired you, but he wants assurance you're not involved in any of these assaults. We keep a good crew here and obey the bricklayer society rules. But you never know what will set off the next hothead."

"I totally understand." William shook his head in agreement. "I've spoken against the violence at meetings and said my peace to plenty of union members." He sighed his words. "It does no good."

Grayson studied him closely. "Well, I think you're a right good chap, Leighton. We don't want any trouble, mind you. I'm just checking where you stand on all this to protect our interests here."

"I appreciate the confidence you have in me," William replied in a firm tone.

"Well, come with me, and I'll introduce you to the crew. There's plenty to do today, so let's get to work."

Thankful he still had a position, William pushed aside the anger for now. He'd deal with Hugh in his way at another time. Right now there was work to do, and that had to be his singular focus. "Slave to none," he whispered to himself. Every workday he repeated the phrase to remind himself one day he would be the employer and master of others and not the worker. With Mary's encouraging words not to underestimate what he could accomplish in life, it gave him the courage to believe. Today would be another brick to lay in the foundation of his dreams.

William sidestepped conflict with most individuals, but when it came to his brother, it was unavoidable. For the majority of his labor that day, he successfully ignored the news about Sheffield. As soon as the opportunity presented itself, he headed straight for Hugh's, seeking the truth about last week's union-sanctioned violence. Tired, he would have much rather gone home, but sleep would have eluded him as he tossed and turned, speculating about what had happened.

As he stood before Hugh's door, he balled his fist and gave it a good pound. The door opened, and he was surprised to see Eliza answer instead.

"William," she gasped.

Straightaway William noticed a bruise on her cheekbone, and Eliza hastily turned her face to the other side.

"Is Hugh home?"

She stood in the doorway, not giving an invitation for him to enter. "No, he's not. Not sure where he is tonight."

Not taking no for an answer, William pushed past her and weaseled his way indoors. The dark interior cast gloomy shadows as only one candle attempted to illuminate the room. He hadn't visited Hugh's residence for quite a while and was appalled at the state of its condition. The place was filthy and reeked of a musty, damp smell. A small fire burned in the stove that looked as if it were about to go out. The interior's contents were unkempt, which surprised William that Eliza had little housekeeping skills or perhaps did not care.

"Is Margaret upstairs?" William glanced in the direction of the dark steps.

"Yes, asleep," Eliza replied. Her voice trembled as

she avoided looking directly at William.

"Do you know where he is, Eliza? I need to talk to him."

"About what?"

"Just union business," William said, trying to make light of his reason. He noted Eliza touch her cheekbone, and William feared the worst.

"Did he do that to you?"

"What?"

"Hit you."

"Oh, this?" She put her hand on her cheek. "No, I walked into the doorjamb, not watching where I was going."

William didn't believe her answer. Hugh had a temper, but he never supposed he would hit his wife in a rage. Upset at the thought of it, he was about to say something when the door flung open and Hugh barged inside. He halted in his step and gawked at William.

"What you doing here?" he slurred.

William smelled alcohol on his breath. Even in the dim light, he could see Hugh's eyes were bloodshot. As he stumbled farther into the room after slamming the door, he braced for the ensuing confrontation. He turned to Eliza, whose eyes widened in fear at her husband's arrival.

"Do you mind giving us a few minutes alone?" William asked in a kindly tone.

She nodded and then proceeded to run up the stairs. When William heard the door close to their bedroom, he reluctantly looked at Hugh.

"You're drunk."

"I'm not that drunk," he said. He swaggered to the

table and flopped onto a wooden chair. "Only drank three ales."

Three was enough to put him over the edge, so William took a chair and sat down next to him.

"Like I said," Hugh reiterated. "What are you doing here?"

"Wanted to let you know I've moved to Broughton and started a new job with Bradshaw and Sons."

"Bloody hell," he yelped. "Just like that you up and move without talking to me."

"I'm telling you now," William blurted in an irritated tone. "Besides, I heard you've been busy." The inference would lead into the conversation William came to discuss anyway. The news about his job, and especially Mary, would have to wait until Hugh was sober and could remember the discussion.

"What news?" Hugh acted indifferent, staring blankly back.

"The attack on Sheffield's. What else?"

"Oh, that news," he slurred. "No news there."

"I want to know one thing, Hugh." William narrowed his eyes at him. "Were you the one who shot the watchman?"

Suddenly his brother broke into a husky, drunken laughter that filled the room. "Yeah, yeah, that was me," he chortled. "I'm such a goddamn bad shot I only hit him in the leg. Should have shot the bastard in the heart 'cause he pointed his gun at me."

William closed his eyes in disbelief as his gut churned into a hard knot. There wasn't an ounce of remorse in Hugh's voice. The man lacked sense and decency. Violence and liquor were the staples of his life. Whether at the union or home, Hugh didn't care who he hurt, including his wife.

The comradery of brotherhood stretched to its limits. As Hugh continued to chuckle about the matter like an immature child, William knew whatever tie that once bound them together, snapped under the weight of disgust.

"You're a bloody fool," he spat, standing upright. "I'm sick of the violence you perpetrate on behalf of the union, and now I see it's come into your own home."

"Now wait a goddamn minute," Hugh bellowed, wobbling to his feet. "What I do behind closed doors is me business, brother, not yours." He took his index finger and poked William in the chest. "And as far as the union goes, I do it for the good of everybody, including you."

Hugh took the flat of his hand and pushed William hard against the shoulder, causing him to stumble backward. Instinctively William balled his fists in defense as anger boiled in his veins at the stupidity of his brother's attitudes.

"You and your high and mighty words," Hugh squawked. "The violence I perp... perpetrated..." He mockingly repeated the words back to his brother, shoving his face in his. "Think you're smarter than everybody else, but you know nothing," he growled.

In a rage, Hugh grabbed a chair and flung it across the floor, splintering one of its legs. "Get the hell out of me home," he bellowed.

"Gladly," William remarked. "I hope the police find out it was you who pulled the trigger. Perhaps a year or two in a cold jail cell might put some sense into that stubborn head of yours, and you'll stop acting like a bloody jackass!"

The words sent Hugh into a shrieking frenzy, flinging obscenities at William, which he never heard come out of his brother's mouth before. Rather than receiving the physical brunt of his anger, William took a quick step toward the door, and Hugh pushed him from behind with a hard shove.

"Get out! Get out!"

A second later, William stepped down the stoop and stumbled into the street. He halted for a moment when Hugh slammed the door behind him with a bang.

At that moment, hatred for his brother choked the air from his lungs. Never had he wrestled with such raw emotions of loathing about one human being. Though Hugh was family, William wanted nothing more to do with him. That morning when he learned of the event from the foreman, his brother's actions dripped shame on his own reputation. Only their separation would cleanse him of that association. If he didn't distance himself now, it would taint the Leighton name forever and the legacy he wanted to leave behind.

As William stomped down the street to make the long trek home, he realized any relationship they once possessed ended that night.

Chapter Fifteen

Every Flower Has a Meaning

As best he could, William forgot the incident with Hugh and settled into his new job. Grayson turned out to be a fair foreman who William found to be far better than Thorpe. The crew at Bradshaw's was a good group of union men that kept to themselves and stayed away from the affairs of those who regularly enforced the rules.

As the attacks continued, the *Manchester Courier* reported on each incident in detail, painting a picture of the union members being nothing more but despots in their own class. William read the report about the Sheffield attack, which had no redeeming qualities. Between the strikes at the cotton mills, the violence of the bricklayers, and the complaints by other trades, relations between laborers and masters strained to a breaking point with threats of more strikes. Manchester had become a hotbed of social instability.

Nevertheless, beyond bricklaying and community unrest, William enjoyed one day a week filled with peace. For the past few Sundays, he met Mary at Miss Beecham's residence. She successfully convinced her uncle that her weekly visits with her former governess were necessary to maintain their friendship. After all, she needed the good counsel of a woman in her life, which her uncle obviously could not provide. He conceded to her request and made no objection to her afternoon teas with Miss Beecham. Of course, little did he know that William joined them on a regular basis.

With the increase in wages, William could afford to bring Mary a small token of his affection. He purchased a bouquet of mixed flowers at a florist, paying particular attention to the choice of blooms. Though he wasn't a botanist by any means, he knew enough that various flowers had meaning. With careful consideration as to the makeup of the gift, he chose flowers that would best speak of his affections, which he had trouble verbalizing in person.

As he clutched the florae in his hand along the way, people smirked at him, knowing he intended to present them to a lady. The business of courting made him look like a fool, but he didn't care. He would give Mary the world if he had it within his means and hoped someday he could.

When he arrived, Mary kept watch for him at the window as usual. Their eyes met, and her lovely smile expressed her excitement. Before he could get to the door, it flung open, and she looked at the gift with delight.

"You brought me flowers?"

William halted in front of her and held out the bunch. He nearly crushed the stems from anticipation. Mary took them in hand and brought the blooms to her nose, sniffing the various selections. Wiser than he thought, she took note of the hidden meanings they held, especially those that expressed love.

"Why, Mr. Leighton," she cooed, looking at him and batting her lashes. "What a thoughtful and expressive gift."

Her perfect appearance in the doorway brought William deep pleasure. The sun danced off the strands of her hair, accenting her hazel eyes to perfection. When her pink lips puckered, understanding the affections he expressed, he lost all sense of propriety. Compelled to act upon his inward longing for Mary, he stepped forward, put his hand gently behind her neck, and drew himself to her lips. A tingling sensation at the touch of her flesh transported him to paradise. When Miss Beecham caught sight of his mischievous conduct, she speedily put an end to it.

"Mr. Leighton!" her voice boomed in his ears. "Kissing Mary in the doorway for the world to see? Have you lost your mind?"

Poor Mary bolted at the sound of Miriam behind her. William answered truthfully.

"Perhaps I have lost my mind," he concluded, wanting to steal another kiss.

"Look, he's brought me flowers." Mary showed the bouquet, and Miriam snatched it out of her hand.

"Good Lord, look at the selection. The man obviously is besotted with you, my dear. Implications of longing and love everywhere between the petals and stems. What will your uncle think? I've never seen so many scandalous flower meanings in one bouquet."

"Oh dear, perhaps I should keep the flowers here and not take them to the vicarage." Mary surmised a wise course of action.

William stood on the stoop and watched both chitchat back and forth as if he no longer existed. "Might I come in?"

"Let the poor man in the door, Mary. I'll go put these in a vase." Miriam walked down the hall with flowers in hand and disappeared.

"Kiss me again while she's gone," Mary begged, looking at him with eagerness in her eyes.

Naturally, he couldn't refuse and took advantage of the moment. Only this time Mary wrapped her arms around his neck and kissed him ardently in return. The blissful sensation of a woman's body flush next to his sent a rush of desire through his veins. He couldn't enjoy the moment any further with the fear of Miriam's soon return, so he pulled away.

"If she catches us again, she'll send me out the door." He chuckled. William grabbed her hand and led her into the parlor, making sure that they sat together on the settee. Being in Mary's presence flooded his heart with peace. As he clutched her hand, he was convinced that he found the perfect companion.

"Oh, William, I must tell you," she gushed. "I've been hired as a clerk at the millinery store in Broughton."

"You have? But what of your uncle? Does he know?"

"Yes, and he's quite furious with me, but I am paying no attention to him. He's pretty much forbidden me to take the job, so Miriam is going to let me stay here until I can find a room in a boarding house nearby the shop."

"The young lady has a mind of her own," Miriam remarked, returning with the flowers arranged nicely in a vase. She set it on a table in front of the window. "Here are your flowers, my dear, full of secret messages tucked between the stems from your fine Mr. Leighton." She turned around with a teasing smirk on her lips. "Now, has he actually said any of these words verbally to you?"

"Miriam!" Mary's cheeks flushed.

"I do love to fiddle with the two of you lovebirds." Miriam chuckled. "Fine, I'll leave you alone—but behave!" She shook a scolding finger at William and then retreated and closed the door.

Mary avoided eye contact during the bantering exchange, but William grew serious in his thoughts. He continued to hold her hand tightly, realizing that he didn't want to live without her in his life.

"She's right," his voice cracked. "I haven't said the words."

Mary turned and beheld him solemnly. Her fingers in the clutch of his hand grew cold, and her breaths rapidly increased. The words had to be spoken because his heart would rupture if he kept it locked up any longer.

"I love you, Mary."

Rather than smiling, her facial expression remained unchanged. For a brief moment he wanted to retract his confession for fear that she did not possess the same devoted emotions. It was a ridiculous thought because she begged for his kiss only minutes ago.

"I love you, William," she whispered in a shaky voice. Her eyes grew moist as if she were on the verge of tears.

Nothing remained left to do but to kiss her again,

and William enjoyed a long and uninterrupted interlude of affection. When he pulled away, he cupped her face in his hands.

"I only have one intention in mind, and that is to marry you when I'm able to care for you properly. Would you mind a long engagement, Mary Booker, or should I wait to ask you what's burning in my heart?"

A nervous giggle escaped her throat as she responded, "I don't mind."

Her answer settled it, and William knew what women expected—romance. He rose to his feet, walked to the flower vase, and pulled out the single orchid in the bouquet. Returning to face Mary, he made the grand gesture that ladies dreamed of and bent down on one knee. With hand outstretched, he offered her the flower of love and spoke the words.

"Mary Booker, would you do me the honor of being my wife?" She gave no hesitation in accepting his offer.

"Yes, Mr. Leighton. I accept your proposal of marriage." She excitedly giggled.

Miriam, who kept a habit of eavesdropping at the door, suddenly burst into the room. "Oh, my heavens, he asked you to marry him? Your father would approve, my dear. Fine young fellow he is, and I know that he will take good care of you."

William rose to his feet, surprised at the affirmative outburst. After all the mocking Miriam had given them in the weeks past, he wasn't sure whether she liked him or not. Her words of verification confirmed his decision to take Mary as his wife.

Miriam ran over and embraced Mary

enthusiastically. "I'm so happy for you, my dear. A winter wedding would do well, don't you think, Mr. Leighton? Yes, a Christmas wedding like your parents once shared."

"Well, that's up to William," Mary answered.

"Christmas," he mused. "Well, it's a goal I can possibly achieve. There are a few good months left of work before the bad weather sets in. I want to make sure I can provide properly for her. You understand."

"Of course I do," Miriam replied. "That is why I like you, Mr. Leighton. You possess the gift of ambition. With Mary by your side, the two of you shall do splendidly together in this life."

"I hope I can live up to your confidence in me," William said sheepishly.

"Now listen, Mary, we'll need to start thinking about your trousseau and wedding dress. What about your uncle? Oh dear, he may balk at the idea of your engagement."

"I'll handle Uncle," Mary announced with confidence in her voice. "Hopefully, William and I can marry elsewhere than Saint George's if he decides to throw a tantrum about our engagement."

"Yes, there are other churches in Broughton," William suggested. "Yet, Mary, it may be best for us both to make peace with your uncle in this matter. After all, he has been your guardian for some time."

After he spoke the words, William thought himself a hypocrite asking Mary to smooth her relations with family, when he had been at bitter odds with his brother. Rather than press the matter, he retracted his statement when he saw it bring grief to her face.

"You do as you please, Mary, and follow your conscience. I shall support your wishes in the matter."

"I'll think about it," she replied.

"Oh, enough of the vicar uncle." Miriam chuckled. "I'm so pleased for a chance to put together a trousseau and find a wedding dress for Mary that I could burst with excitement."

The path to marriage lay before William. After the years of bachelorhood and no interest in finding a mate, he finally came to the place where his life's path would alter. Marriage meant not only companionship with the woman he loved but also the possibility of children and the building of a family. The pressure to provide would increase tenfold, but he felt strong, confident, and able to face the challenges that lay ahead.

Perhaps Christmas would be an excellent time to wed and begin that journey.

Chapter Sixteen

THE CALLING CARD

A new infusion of confidence sent William out into the street as an engaged man. The world looked different, and he finally understood why a bloke could lose his good sense when it came to a female.

He stuck his hand into his pocket and fingered the calling card that Mr. Cooper gave him months ago. Today would be a good day to visit, so he pulled it out and noted the address again, which was down Oxford Road past the Manchester Royal Infirmary. Because of the distance, he took an omnibus to a stop where he could easily walk the remainder of the way.

The terraced home was situated in a decent neighborhood but didn't speak to any significant wealth. William halted for a moment second-guessing why he had come and then reminded himself that with marriage came responsibility. Perhaps there would be better opportunities behind the door in front of where he stood.

He gave the knocker a good rap and waited. It seemed like an eternity as he heard nothing more than silence. One more time he knocked and waited. When he was about to give up, the door opened and Mr. Cooper stood looking at him with evident surprise on his face.

"Good gracious, Leighton. You didn't forget about my invitation."

Surprised that he remembered his name, William grinned. "I hope my unannounced arrival is not an imposition, Mr. Cooper."

"No, no," he said, throwing the door wide open. "Come in. I'm most pleased to see you."

William removed his hat and stepped into the foyer. The interior was clean and well lit, with elegant furnishing and other décor.

"Come into the parlor," Mr. Cooper said, leading the way. "Can I get you anything to drink? Whiskey perhaps?"

Not much of a drinking man when it came to hard liquor, especially on Sunday, William politely declined. "No, thank you."

"Well, hope you don't mind if I pour myself a few fingers," he remarked. He walked to a glass decanter, pulled the stopper, and poured an inch of whiskey into the bottom of a crystal glass. "Well, sit down, man, and tell me what you've been up to."

William didn't like to discuss his private affairs with strangers, so he kept the personal aspects of his life protected except for work.

"I'm working now at Bradshaw's in Broughton, bricklaying on new homes."

"Broughton, you say?"

"Yes, after we spoke, I visited the area to look at the fields you mentioned."

"So what did you think?"

"Fine place to start a business, Mr. Cooper."

"Reggie. Call me Reggie, and I hope you don't

mind me calling you William."

Surprised at the quick informality, William felt slightly awkward but conceded to his request. "Have you decided to proceed with your idea?"

Reggie gulped the alcohol in his glass and then set it down on a side table. "The negotiations with the landowners in the area have gone well. We've agreed upon a price to lease the fields, and I've purchased a plot of land for a building to house the apparatus and set up office."

"Congratulations, that's wonderful news," William exclaimed, genuinely happy that the man's plans were progressing.

"I ordered the brickmaking machine from London, and it will be here by the first of January." His face turned sour. "But I'll be honest with you. I'm worried after reading about what happened to Sheffield's." He paused. "I'm assuming you heard about it."

William suddenly had a taste for a swig of whiskey. Sullied by his association with the union, naturally certain members reflected poorly on him personally. Of late, he even avoided going to the meetings so he wouldn't see Hugh.

"Yes, I heard about it."

"Well, you're a union man, what say you about all this? Can't these men see that these inventions are good and not as evil as they think they are?" Reggie shook his head. "It's ignorance, as far as I'm concerned. Plain ignorance." He paused shortly and looked apologetically at William. "I mean no disrespect to you, but you impress me as an intelligent and educated man who knows better than to be suspicious of progress."

At that moment, William felt as if he were being pressed into the form of a brick. After all, it was his livelihood, his coworkers, his union, his trade heritage for goodness' sake. He hated to speak ill of other people to another human being, but he couldn't agree more. Was his class nothing more than the tyrants they had been made out to be by the newspapers? There were labeled terrorists as the disgraces continued. Yes, he was both proud of his trade and embarrassed of it as well.

"Ignorance is a strong word," he said thoughtfully. "Men's actions are often driven by fear, and that is what incites the violence. They fear change and losing their jobs, which leads to anxiety about destitution and the inability to care for families." William paused and furrowed his brow. "I've known that fear in my own childhood and still struggle to this day not to let it get the better of me."

"Tell me truthfully, William, have you ever been involved in the violence?"

Reggie leaned in William's direction, staring into his eyes. The question surprised him, but the man had the right to know whom he would be dealing with if anything came of their association.

"Never, and I don't intend to either," he emphatically replied. "But changing the minds of those who don't understand any other way is not an easy task."

"Well, regardless." He sighed. "Perhaps I'm mad to take the risk, and I've taken the step with some apprehension. By January, I'll be in business in Broughton off of Fairy Lane." He looked pointedly at

William. "I'm going to need help. I have the commercial savvy to handle those affairs and get contracts, but the hiring of men and handling the day-to-day operations is going to take a foreman I can trust."

"You need someone who understands the working of the machinery, that's for sure. I'm not that man, I'm afraid."

"Well, I'm sure we can hire a mechanic who understands all those engines, gears, and levers," he commented. "Those machines form twenty to twenty-five thousand bricks a day, and all we need is two men and four lads to help run it and a hearty crew in the brickfields, a man or two for shifts on the kiln, and storage."

William's eyes widened at the count. It was astronomical. "My God, that's a lot of bricks. I had no idea of the output."

"Well, there's plenty of work out there, William. Construction is everywhere with warehouses, terraced homes, factories, workhouses, and the talk of a new town hall, not to mention a new prison. A man could make a fortune off the contract of the town hall alone."

"Indeed." William concurred, excited at the prospects.

"But then again, I don't want any trouble with the union. The possibility of being the next firebombed business after I've invested my entire inheritance into it makes me sick. Change must come about, or no master brickmakers will succeed in Manchester or Salford. We will all go broke or quit the trade."

Cooper was right, but how to affect change would

not be easy. Fleetingly he considered returning to the meetings and broaching the subject to lift the restrictions. With all the new inventions, the union certainly couldn't bomb every master who purchased the machine to make bricks. It was a ridiculous notion.

They both fell into a digestive silence, mulling over their conversation. A minute later, William offered another suggestion.

"Eventually master brickmakers should form their own association for clout with the unions."

"Good idea, but I think there is more than can be accomplished with men like you being influencers in the union for change. You strike me as a man who has the power of persuasion in your speech."

William laughed. "Well, if I do, I've not used it to my advantage yet."

"I'll tell you what," Reggie said. "Come the first of January, I want you working for me as a foreman. I'll pay you twice or three times as much what you're making now to start."

Aghast at the offer, William didn't quite know how to respond. "That is extremely generous of you, but you are hardly acquainted with me, sir."

Cooper gazed at him intently as if he were affirming his gut decision. After a few moments, he spoke. "I'm a good judge of character and possess no qualms about my assessment of you." He halted a moment, and eagerness raised his brow. "So what say you?"

William was about to answer when the door opened and a woman entered with a young girl at her side. She walked into the parlor, and he rose to his feet.

"Ah, my wife," Reggie said. "Home from church." He leaned into William. "I'm not much of a churchgoer." He got up and walked to the woman, who took off her hat and held it in her hand. Reggie towered above her petite frame. Dressed in a blue frock and hat, her brown locks cascaded in circular curls down her back, making her look like a regal lady.

"I see we have company," she said, eyeing William. "Who is this, husband?"

"William, I'd like to introduce you to my lovely wife, Justine." He put his hand on the shoulder of the young girl who looked to be about three years of age. "This pretty little thing is Ann Marie."

"Pleasure to meet you," William replied. The young family together in their home gave him a rush of excitement at what awaited him in the years to come.

"Justine, this is William Leighton. We've been discussing business, and he's been giving me advice."

"Oh, do you own a business as well?" Justine looked at him curiously.

"Not yet, I'm afraid," he responded. "I admire your husband's tenacity, though, to start one by himself."

"I'm trying my best to convince this young man to come work for me, but I'm not sure my persuasion is doing the trick."

"And are you married, Mr. Leighton?"

Surprised at the personal question, Reggie gave his wife a cockeyed look. "A little personal, dear," he reminded her in a kind tone.

"Well, I'm happy to say that as of today, a young

lady accepted my proposal of marriage." William shoved out his chest with an air of pride.

"I'll be damned," Reggie exclaimed. "Why didn't you say so earlier?"

"Dear, don't swear in front of our daughter." Justine rebuked her husband. She put her arm around Ann Marie, who stood in this midst of them quietly watching the conversational exchange. The child appeared well mannered, to say the least.

"Congratulations," Reggie said. "More the reason to accept my offer to help me get this business off the ground." He put his hand on William's shoulder and looked him straight in the eye. "What say you? Will you be my foreman come the first of January?"

"You better say yes, Mr. Leighton, or he will hound you until you relent. My husband never takes no for an answer." Justine smiled warmly at him.

William couldn't think of any reason to refuse the offer. Sure, he'd miss laying bricks, but this would be a chance to be a foreman—a definite step in the right direction. He would have to purchase a bowler hat to look the part and decided he'd look quite dapper in one.

"I accept your offer, Mr. Cooper," he replied, posing his hand for a shake.

"Good! I feel it in my gut, Leighton, we're going to make a great team together."

"Well, now that's settled," Justine said. "I'll make us some tea." She took Ann Marie's hand. "Come on, sweetie, and I'll get you some biscuits."

William settled back into the chair, aghast that everything moved so swiftly. He told himself that he made the right choice even though he knew little about Reggie Cooper. On the surface, the man appeared decent enough. He possessed business sense, ambition, and a wife and child. In the few hours that they spent together talking, William trusted his intuition that Cooper was a decent bloke. The timing couldn't be more perfect. He would wed Mary at Christmas and be more than able to support a household.

"William, I'm thinking of selling here and moving to Broughton as well. Cheetham Street has some nice properties owned by the landowners. I may convince them to sell a plot to build myself a residence after the business gets up and running."

"Good area," William responded, dreaming that one day he would build something to call his own.

Justine returned with the tea, and William settled comfortably in the chair to spend more time with Reggie. The day had been full of proposals—one to wed and another a job. He couldn't be happier.

Chapter Seventeen

THE BATTLE FIELD

After reflecting on Reggie's statement regarding his influence on the union, William decided to attend the next meeting. Hugh would almost certainly be there as well, and William intended to go out of his way to avoid a confrontation. There were others, like William, who were not in total agreement regarding the violence. To have some comradery at the gathering, he sought out the men that were conservative in their views regarding the use of force. The individuals he had in mind were Jeremy Wood and George Mason.

When he approached the door of the assembly hall, Pickett, the current secretary, stood at the entrance, checking off names. It was unusual because the doors were always open and individuals just streamed into the assembly hall to find a chair.

"Ah, Leighton, I see you're here," he noted, going down the list and placing a check by his name.

"Taking roll tonight?" William looked at him cockeyed. "Is this something new?"

"Well, the newspaper journalists have been sneaking into our meetings, then reporting in the papers what's been said. We're trying to put a stop to it. What we do is none of their damn business," he grumbled.

"I see."

With all the negative articles regarding the unions in the papers, no doubt the leadership attempted to stifle the stream of information. William surmised it to be a lost cause because there were always snitches in their midst who, if they were brave enough, would report business behind closed doors for a few shillings.

As he entered the room, he glanced around and saw Wood standing with Mason. They appeared to be in a discussion. William approached and greeted them.

"Mind if I join?"

"You're welcome, Leighton, but I'm afraid not your brother." Wood nodded to the front of the room where Hugh stood with his usual gang.

As soon as William glanced at him, his stomach turned sour. The sad state of affairs of their estrangement lay heavily upon his heart.

"I doubt my brother would care to join us," William remarked. "Do you know what's on the agenda tonight?"

"One order of business is Pickett is retiring as secretary," Mason replied.

"What's the reason?" William asked, interested in the gossip behind it all.

"Not sure."

"I doubt it's his conscience." Wood chuckled. "Being the keeper of all those meeting notes must be draining."

Wood leaned into William. "So rumor has it your

brother shot the watchman, is that true? We were just talking about the incident. Mason thinks one of these days someone is going to get killed."

Shocked that the information about Hugh's involvement had already made the rounds, he hesitated to confirm or deny the fact. He hated lying about anything, so he skirted the question.

"I agree if the violence continues, someone will get killed. It could be one of the enforcers rather than a watchman." As he concluded the sentence, the president called the meeting to order. Thankfully, he didn't have to answer the inquiry. Regardless, he could tell by the look on their faces they believed Hugh had done the deed.

"All right, take your seats and stop the jabbering. We've got a lot to cover," bellowed Harrison over their heads.

William's eyes drifted to Hugh. They avoided each other until that moment as he caught him in a brooding gaze directed his way.

"The offenses against the union's rules continue to plague Manchester. We have masters refusing to pay men who walk any distance to work as part of the day's labor. They think we need to set limits as to how many miles they should compensate for walking to work." Harrison sniggered. "Too many of you lads believe that walking a few miles out of your way to the pub after work should be compensated by your bosses."

"Damn right," one man yelled above the crowd. A roar of laughter rose from the members.

"We'll consider the matter further if we should set mileage limits on the compensation." He stood at the podium and flipped over another piece of paper.

"All right, boys. The main topic of discussion tonight is brickmaking machines. What say you? Shall we continue to enforce the rules no bricks made by those contraptions can be used in construction in Manchester? Frankly, I still consider them a threat to our livelihood."

"Hear, hear!" The majority of the members screamed aloud.

Surprisingly another member rose to his feet. "Frankly, I don't see what the problem is. You can't stop progress by destroying every brickmaker's use of the machines." His comment garnered grumbling throughout the hall.

"The damn things steal our jobs!" a voice rang out in the crowd. "Handmade bricks are of better quality."

Unable to remain silent, William's voice rang out. "I don't believe you see the bigger picture." He stood to his feet. Surprisingly, everyone turned their eyes on him, some of which contained daggers flying his way. "The city is growing, and the need for bricks is increasing. Brickmaking machines output more bricks than handmade and can handle the increase in demand. We hurt ourselves by not allowing them because they actually produce more work in the long run. No one is going to lose jobs if we allow their use."

Suddenly Hugh jumped to his feet and pointed directly at him. "Lads, me brother here is a dreamer." The majority of the attendees laughed in unison. "He seems to think that these contraptions are our friends when in fact they are monsters out to destroy our living!" A large group of men rose to their feet in agreement, shaking their fists in the air in support and howling, "Hear, hear!"

William stood his ground. His heart pounded in his throat as he spoke. "My brother has admitted many a time, including in the presence of some members here, that he is the brawn of the family while I am the brains." A rumbling grumble flowed through the crowd, and eyes shot back and forth at them. "Since he has repeatedly admitted that fact, I once again assert these machines are not our enemies. Wisdom dictates that they will increase work opportunities because the quotas for bricks in new construction will be met."

As soon as the words left his lips, Hugh bolted in his direction, but the men by his side prevented him from going any farther than a few feet. His public act of hatred pounded another nail of discord between them, and William watched as the audience reacted. Wood and Mason stood to their feet along William's side. Wood's voice boomed throughout the room.

"I concur with William on this matter. There is a direct correlation between the number of bricks produced to the need in the Manchester district lines. No bricks available for construction mean no work for us! Think about it, lads. To fight against the ability to meet demand is foolish."

"Hear, hear!" Mason agreed.

As the crowd became more unruly, the president took control. "All right, all right, your voices have been heard. Take your seats and settle down before we end up brawling like a bunch of drunks at the pub." William glanced at his brother, who sat down appearing as angry as a stampeding bull.

"It's been a hearty discussion on the matter, and

we will keep it in mind," Harrison added. "I thank our learned and brainy union member, Mr. Leighton here, for his input, but it doesn't mean by any stretch we are ready to forgo the restrictions. I'm a firm believer at this point the machines are injurious to our trade."

Those in agreement applauded. Harrison turned the subject to the secretary's retirement and the upcoming vacancy to be filled. The next assembly individuals would be nominated and votes cast.

"I think that concludes this meeting." Harrison glanced at Hugh and William and then jeered. "I suggest the Leighton brothers keep their distance as they exit the building."

William rose to his feet, along with Wood and Mason. "Thanks for the vote of confidence."

"I agree, William," Wood remarked. "Their hatred of progress only hurts us all."

Mason put his hand on William's shoulder. "Wood and I will flank you on the way out," he said in a solemn tone. "I believe a few of the members would like to shove the pointed tip of a trowel in your back."

As William saw the looks thrown his way, he made no objection to the friends at his side. When they stepped outdoors, the fresh air cooled his heated flesh. It only took a minute for Hugh to approach and declare his loathing.

"Watch your back, brother." Hugh hissed. "Making enemies in the flanks of the union can get you killed."

Even though Hugh stood six inches above William's frame, he shoved out his chest like a young lion. "Is that a threat, brother?" he snarled in return.

"You can take it however you want."

One of Hugh's comrades grabbed him by the arm and dragged him away. "Come on, Hugh," he encouraged. "Not here."

Wood's mouth gaped open at the exchange. "I didn't know you two had such a falling out," he morosely noted. "Most realize you don't agree eye to eye, but when did this animosity come about?"

William seethed inwardly at the situation. "After the last attack," he grumbled. There had been no admittance on his part of Hugh's involvement, but he expressed why.

"Well, I doubt he'd really kill you," Mason said. "You two have thicker blood than that after all these years."

"Perhaps," William responded. "The rift between us only widens, and frankly I see no way to repair it at this point." Exhausted about the evening's events, William offered a handshake to the two men. "I suppose I'll see you at the next meeting if I'm still alive." He sniggered.

They shook his hand in return, and William walked down the street teaming with other men on their way home. He was about four miles from his flat, and the omnibuses had stopped running. Frankly, he needed a long walk to burn off the anger still flowing through his veins about his brother's stupidity and the rest of the union members.

It was hard to believe they would ever come around, but now he held a vested interest in turning their attitudes favorably toward the machines. With Mr. Cooper investing his future income, it would do no good to have thousands of machine-made bricks on hand that couldn't be sold or used in the Manchester city limits. It presented a conundrum that needed solving, and William wasn't quite sure what it would take to turn the tide of protest.

He shoved his hands into his pants pocket and wandered down the gas-lighted street toward Broughton, hoping for a restful sleep and dreams of Mary.

Chapter Eighteen

THE BLESSING

The weeks passed, and William focused on his new job while spending time with Mary at Miss Beecham's on Sundays. In the meantime, Mary took the advice and applied for a clerk's position at the millinery shop and had been hired to tend customers three days a week. When she told her uncle, he wasn't too pleased with her decision as it would take her from the vicarage and her responsibilities at home.

In spite of his objection, Mary asserted her independence and moved in with Miss Beecham, who she planned to live with until their wedding. While William laid bricks, Mary set hats on the heads of ladies and enjoyed her newfound endeavor. He was proud of her accomplishments.

Eventually, though, she had a change of heart regarding her uncle. After speaking about it at some length, they decided to meet with him after service on Sunday to let him know of their engagement.

As they arrived at the vicarage, William hesitated for a moment and faced Mary. "How will you handle it if he forbids the marriage?"

"He can forbid nothing," she announced. "I'm quite happy with Miss Beecham's approval of you as my husband. I barely had a relationship with uncle before my father died, so I owe him nothing more than the courtesy of informing him of our wedding."

Satisfied that Mary would not be dissuaded, they knocked on the door with determination in their hearts. When it opened, a stout, plump woman answered the door. She displayed cherry-colored cheeks, bright eyes, wild red hair twisted into a bun on top of her head. With a straight face, she greeted them.

"Yes?"

"Who are you?" Mary asked.

"Mrs. Goodson, young lady, I'm the vicar's new housekeeper." She puffed out her chest like a peacock marking territory, spouting a clear Irish accent.

"Oh, I see," Mary replied, smirking at her brazen response.

Her uncle rounded the corner. "You can go, Mrs. Goodson, and get us a pot of tea and some cakes." She scurried off, and he turned his attention to them.

"Hmm," he mused aloud. "I see the two of you have come together as a force of one to speak to me." He eyed them up and down with a lifted brow and then stepped aside. "Come inside and tell me what's on your mind."

Mary and William entered into the small foyer. The door closed, and Mary stepped forward and kissed her uncle on the cheek.

"A kiss is it?" He snorted. "You must want something." He motioned to the parlor. "Come in and sit down, and let's talk."

"When did you get a housekeeper?" Mary inquired.

"After you left, I had no woman in the house to cook and clean. I have a church to run, so I needed help."

He pointed to the settee, and they sat down together. William let out a nervous sigh because he wanted things to go well. His estranged relationship with his brother had been hard enough that he didn't wish Mary to experience a torn relationship with her uncle. He glanced at her clutching her hands together in her lap, noting her own uneasiness about the situation. They agreed beforehand that he would do the talking, so he inhaled a breath and spoke.

"We wanted to let you know that Mary and I have formed an attachment over the past months."

"Have you now?" John reacted with a raised brow. "And how far has this attachment, as you call it, progressed?"

"I'm engaged to William," Mary proudly announced, interjecting into the conversation. They watched his reaction as the vicar studied them like they were a page in his Bible, searching for truth. He looked directly at Mary.

"I'm not surprised, my dear, as it was obvious the first day you lay eyes upon this young man that you had designs on him."

Mary's cheeks flushed. "I know that I fell in love with him the first time I saw him attend service," she admitted sheepishly. Her hand reached over and grabbed William's cold fingers.

"And what about you, Leighton? When did your affections toward my niece become evident?" John leaned in toward him with narrowed eyes. William knew he better not skirt around the subject but be truthful.

"I'll admit, at first I was reluctant to let my heart wander toward your niece because I feared I wasn't good enough for the young lady."

"Oh, William," Mary replied, looking sadly at him.

"But I've done well for myself and can provide for her now. She has become the center of my world." He chuckled somewhat. "Actually, she's good for me as she encourages and believes in my dreams for the future." William paused for a moment and squeezed her hand. "I love her, sir. We want to get married Christmas week and have come for your blessing."

The room grew deadly silent as John mulled over the announcement. At first William could not ascertain if he approved or disapproved by the ordinary look on his face. As the seconds slipped by into minutes without a word spoken, he feared the worst. Mary's facial expression displayed her own anxiety when her uncle closed his eyes. William wondered if he were praying for heavenly intervention. Finally, as they gazed at each other in worry, John spoke.

"How do you intend to provide for my niece, might I ask? And where will you live?"

Without hesitation, William announced the news. "As of January the first, I have a new position as a foreman at a brickmaking company. My salary is such that Mary and I shall be able to rent a terraced house on Fenney Street in Broughton."

John reacted with eyes widened at the news. "Well, I'm impressed," he said in a jovial voice. "Apparently you have left me no recourse but to give you and my niece my blessing."

"Oh, Uncle," Mary screeched. "Thank you."

"Now, I'm assuming that Miss Beecham has been intricately involved in this little affair. Will she help you, my dear, with the details of the wedding? You need a lady to guide you in these matters."

"Yes, Uncle, she has been more than helpful already." Mary flashed an impish grin.

"Will you wed here at Saint George's or elsewhere?"

William and Mary discovered a picturesque church in Prestwich, only a few miles from where they would reside. Because of its grand interior and a history dating back to the thirteenth century, Mary fell in love with it straightaway, begging William to use the location. He agreed it would be an excellent place to start their lives together.

"I hope you will not be offended, vicar, but we have chosen the Church of Saint Mary the Virgin in Prestwich to wed," he replied.

"Ah, I see. It's a beautiful stately church. Have you spoken with Father Bartlett?"

"Not yet. We wanted to wait until we spoke with you," Mary replied.

"Well, I'm a bit sad that it shall not happen at Saint George's, but it's your decision, Mary, and I accept it if that is what you wish."

"You will come to the wedding, won't you?" she asked.

"Yes, but I insist on having a wedding reception here at the vicarage. Will you at least agree to a wedding breakfast? I'm sure my new housekeeper and cook will be more than happy to oblige.

"You might ask me first," she scoffed, walking in

with a tray, pot of tea, and cups. "Are these the two lovebirds you spoke about?" She eyed them playfully. "Your niece is as pretty as a peach."

"Oh, Uncle, you don't have to go to any trouble," Mary assured him with a tone of guilt.

"No trouble, dearie," Miss Goodson countered. "No trouble at all. If there's any trouble to be had, it's with Father Booker here for not asking me first."

William and Mary laughed at her bantering. John rolled his eyes.

"I'm afraid I should have asked for more references before I hired her," he replied with a giggle. "She does more than cook and clean around here. I'm always in trouble about something."

"Huh!" Miss Goodson snickered, leaving the room. "The good Lord put me here to watch over you."

Suddenly John rose to his feet and approached as they sat on the settee together. Gently he laid his hand upon their heads.

"Bless this couple, Lord, in their union, and give them a lifetime of happiness." John's voice cracked as he spoke, and he stepped back and observed them with pleasure.

William got up and offered a handshake. "Thank you, sir."

Mary likewise approached and gave her uncle a hug. The sight of reconciliation about the matter brought joy to William's heart. It would only add to her happiness on their wedding day.

"Well then, let's have some tea and cakes so I can at least give you some marital advice before the big day." His eyes sparkled mischievously.

William and Mary sat in Father Bartlett's office, watching him flip through his diary on his desk. They glanced at each other with hopeful eyes that he could accommodate their request. It was the middle of October, and they needed the three months before a date in December for the reading of the wedding banns.

"It appears that you are in luck. The church is available Monday morning the twentieth, but I'm afraid that I am not." He looked up at them sitting in front of his desk. "My wife has committed me to visit her parents in Liverpool until Christmas Eve."

"Oh dear," Mary moaned. "You mean you cannot marry us?"

"I'm afraid not," he said, shaking his head.

A sinking sensation drained William from the inside, and he imagined that Mary felt the same awfulness.

"Nevertheless, I've spoken with your uncle already, as he advised me that you would be visiting. He has agreed to officiate the ceremony on Monday morning, the twentieth of December here at Saint Mary's." He folded his hands and placed them on the desk.

"Thank goodness," Mary exclaimed, reaching over and squeezing William's hand.

Relieved that their plans were coming to fruition, William sighed.

"Now, you've come to me just in time," Father Bartlett continued. "As you are aware, the marriage banns must be read of your intention to marry before the congregation. The purpose, of course, is to inquire if any person believes the marriage may not lawfully take place, in addition to giving the congregation the opportunity to pray for you in the coming months." His face turned serious. "Do either of you know of any reason you cannot marry?"

"None," William replied without hesitancy.

"I know of none," Mary agreed.

"Well, you are both of age, so we shall marry you on the twentieth of December, eighteen hundred and sixty-six the year of our Lord."

"Thank you," William said.

"Now, I do require a few sessions of private instruction for you both to attend before you complete your vows. Marriage is a solemn act in the eyes of God and not to be taken lightly."

Smiling at Mary, he remembered the somewhat comical advice they received from her uncle. With a bit of luck, the vicar of this parish would be more somber in his instruction. Whatever the lesson, he would take heed; but as he glanced at Mary, he knew in his heart they would get along just fine.

They said their goodbyes and walked outdoors into the autumn air. The leaves on the trees turned hues of red and gold. A slight breeze rustled the branches. They held hands and strolled through the grassy areas of the churchyard, walking between the slabs of graves that dated back to the sixteen hundreds.

William took note of the landscape, descending into a field of green grass. The church captured his fancy too because of the scenery that brought peace and tranquility. He would marry at this location, but he wondered what else Saint Mary's would become in his lifetime. Perhaps babies would be baptized here, and in his old age, he would be buried here. The sobering thought bothered him, and he halted a moment and faced Mary.

"I'm going to kiss you, Mary Booker, in this churchyard," he announced. He slipped his arm around her waist and drew her near.

"Well, there isn't a soul around except for the ones in the ground, and I doubt they will care if you kiss me or not."

He chuckled at her odd humor and brought his lips to hers. The notion of their wedding night had been steadily on his mind. Although William had never been with a woman intimately, he felt sure, even without Hugh's advice, he would do fine consummating their marriage. As he teased her mouth with his tongue, Mary pulled away in astonishment.

"Why, William Leighton," she scolded him. "What are you doing?"

Horrified that he might have offended her by his playfulness, he grimaced. "Kissing you."

"What will these corpses think?" She giggled at him and tightened her embrace around his neck.

William could tell by the sparkle in her eye that she didn't mind, so the next few minutes they kissed while standing among the dead. Strangely, William had never felt so alive and at peace.

Chapter Nineteen

GRAVEYARD OF BITTERNESS

Hugh stood by his mother's unmarked grave with a makeshift wooden cross in hand. He shoved the pointed end into the ground far enough to keep the memorial upright. As he stepped back and focused on his simple creation, it appeared insignificant in a graveyard with grand monuments and inscriptions. Regardless, at least the place where she lay had been marked with the symbol she believed in, but he did not.

He stared at the ground that grassed over from the day the hole had been dug for her wooden coffin. A part of his conscience struggled with guilt for refusing to take her in, thinking it might have kept her alive longer. Nothing could be done about it now as her body decomposed and returned to the earth. If heaven did exist, he hoped she arrived at a place of peace. Otherwise, if the church's teachings were nothing more than fairy tales, living a life in this tiresome world had no meaning except labor and heartache.

Eliza told him a month ago she carried another child. His relentless attempts in spite of her indifference paid off. At first he feared being overjoyed in case she lost the baby. As her belly rounded, it confirmed that another mouth was on its way to be fed. He hoped it was a boy.

Last week a letter finally arrived from his elder brother, Aaron. Hugh asked Pickett at the union to read it to him. Aaron couldn't read or write either and must have found another person to scribble out the words for him.

Unfortunately, his elder brother had no inkling about his mother's death because he had been at sea for months. Since Hugh wasn't on speaking terms with William, any correspondence would have to wait unless Pickett would write a letter for him in return.

Apparently, Aaron landed safely with his wife and children. He sought work in the family trade of bricklaying and hoped to settle in the new land that Hugh couldn't imagine. The stories about its landscape and strange animals that jumped around on their back legs left odd visions in his head. Hugh didn't quite know what they looked like, having never seen a picture of a kangaroo. Sadly, he would never see Aaron or his children again but accepted that his choice to leave had been based on the hope of a better life.

Hugh continued to stand at the grave with his hands shoved in his pocket and his head bowed. As his thoughts wandered, he heard a male voice from behind.

"We don't usually allow markers on this side of the church."

Hugh swung around and came face-to-face with the vicar. Instantly he scowled at the man and wanted to sling a mouthful of curses in his face.

"But for you and your brother, I will make an

exception," he replied in a sincere tone. The answer tempered Hugh's anger.

"Good, because I wasn't about to remove it if you said no."

"Understandable." The vicar took a step closer and came to Hugh's side. "How are the preparations for the wedding coming along?"

Hugh swung his head and looked at him, scrunching his brows together in confusion. "What wedding?"

"Well, your brother's, of course."

Shocked at the news, Hugh turned away, not wanting the vicar to see the pained expression on his face. "Didn't know 'bout any wedding. We don't talk much these days."

"William hadn't mentioned to me when my niece and he visited that you were not on speaking terms."

"You mean he's marrying your niece?"

"Yes, Mary," the vicar responded. "I'm happy for them. They make a fine couple."

"Well, I'll be damned." Hugh sighed, not caring if the vicar scoffed at his language. "Didn't think he'd know what to do with a woman." Even though they sorely disagreed about union matters, Hugh admitted the news did bring him an ounce of pleasure. "So when's the wedding?"

"Monday the twentieth of December at Saint Mary's in Prestwich."

"Why the bloody hell way over there?" The vicar raised his brow at his continued vulgar language. "Oh, never mind. He mentioned he was moving to Broughton."

"Perhaps you and your wife will get an invitation

to the joyous affair. I'll be marrying them myself."

"Don't hold your breath, vicar," Hugh replied. "Even if I did, I'm not inclined to see him."

"I'm sorry to hear of it, Mr. Leighton. A dose of forgiveness is better than the bitterness of discord, especially when it comes to family."

Hugh didn't like the man's remark and became indignant. "Don't go preaching at me. I'm no believer in your god. Religion is a waste of me time." He stepped away to put distance between them. "I best be going now," he grumbled. Hugh headed for the street.

"Any words of congratulations that I can convey to William?" the vicar called after him.

"Nothing from me." The cruel words shot from his lips, and he stomped down the path in a foul mood. When they were on speaking terms, Hugh couldn't wait to see William married. He teased him enough about his bachelorhood, and their mother would have found pleasure in seeing him find a sweet girl. The vicar's niece probably shared all of William's high and mighty values, making them a good pair.

Briefly he wondered how William's new work situation turned out. Out of curiosity, he made sure that Bradshaw Builders were following the union rules regarding employees and the use of bricks. Lucky for William, they seemed to be on the up-and-up, which was a good thing for his brother. If he ever had the gumption to do otherwise with another company that didn't adhere to the union's edicts, he would have no qualms of making sure that he personally enforced the matter himself.

With the pub in sight, he headed for the back

room to meet up with the council to discuss the latest infractions in the district. Hugh's time had been increasingly consumed with union matters, having become a delegate for the society. His extra activities in the dead of night continued to supplement his income.

Directed to the room where the men gathered, Hugh opened the door to see eight of the thirteen men on the council who arrived. They included Brown, Stapleton, Barstow, Whitaker, Britten, Simpson, Moss, and Potts sitting at a table. Brown usually led the committee gatherings, which were less informal than the union meetings in the assembly hall.

"We were about to start without you," Brown said, appearing irritated at Hugh's late arrival.

"Sorry, got waylaid by a vicar, if you can believe that story." Hugh chuckled and took a chair.

"You don't have an ounce of religion in you," Stapleton balked in a mocking tone. "What the hell you talking about?"

"At me mother's grave," Hugh answered. "Forget about it." He glanced at Brown, who shuffled some papers on the tabletop. "So what's on the agenda?"

"A list of violations with warning letters to issue and enforcements as needed."

Stapleton could read and write, so he sat ready with paper, pen, and inkwell to start scribbling notes.

"First on the list is Wild. He discharged four union men for drunkenness. I guess they went on a drinking binge and were absent for three days. Wild discharged them. They came to the union asking that we advocate on their behalf, so Mr. Potts here visited the workplace." Brown snickered. "You know how intimidating he can get when riled up, and he demanded that Wild hire the men back, but he refused."

"Bastard spit his answer in me face with clenched teeth," Potts retorted. "I don't take kindly to spit."

"Point taken," Stapleton replied.

"Then the man had the gall to say he'd rather set the bricks himself than to bring back the drunks on the job," Potts grumbled. "I told him if he laid a hand on any brick, he'd be fined by the union two pounds ten shillings. I told him the rule of the trade is no one is allowed to set a brick who is not a union brick setter."

"And what did he say to that?" Moss asked.

"The bastard laughed."

Stapleton frowned. "I think a formal letter of warning from the committee is forthcoming that if he doesn't hire back the men he discharged, the union will support his crew striking until he does. If he attempts to set bricks by himself for the housing project they are currently working on, then we will charge the monetary penalty. If he refuses to pay, then we'll discuss the proper retribution for the offense."

Hugh sat and listened to the stack of infringements that continued to plague the Manchester district. As far as he was concerned, the masters and contractors were nothing but thieves of the trade. If it weren't for the journeymen bricklayers, Manchester would crumble in development.

"We have another report of a master brickmaker, Marsten, who has in his employ no union men. The president has concurred that we should initiate a destruction of bricks on his site. Any volunteers?"

"I'm up for it," Hugh replied. "Frankly, I feel like punching a few walls in the mood I'm in."

Potts spoke up. "I got a few of the regular union lads looking to make a few quid. What are you paying for this job?"

"I'll discuss it with the secretary, and Hugh will give you the money, as usual, to see it's taken care of."

"When you want the job done?"

"Next week should suffice," Stapleton said. "Is Kip still available should we need a few beatings?"

Britten replied. "Yes, ten pounds is still his rate. Should I contact him for another job?"

"Not yet," Stapleton remarked. "We still have the matter on the books regarding Pickering using his son, and he's not a union man. Give him a few more warnings personally, Potts, and if he doesn't comply, let's hire Kip to give his son a good beating."

"Will do, but the man's stubborn as hell and will most likely refuse," Potts answered.

"Now, regarding the last union meeting and brickmaking machines. We have no rules against machine-made bricks—at least printed," he clarified. "Regardless, any builder who uses them, union men are not supposed to work with him."

"Don't get me started," Hugh interjected with narrowed eyes.

"One of our informants has advised me that a new order has gone through to Bradley & Craven for a new brickmaking machine."

"Not another one," Barstow moaned, pulling his mouth to one side.

"A man, whose name is unfamiliar to me, Mr. Reginald Cooper, has put in the order. Supposedly he's setting up a new business in Higher Broughton, of all places, off of Fairy Lane."

"When's this coming about?" Hugh inquired, suddenly interested after hearing the location.

"Sometime early next year. I don't have any other details," Stapleton replied.

Brown interjected. "Well, it's too early to say if it's much of a threat where it's located or how much business he'll do. Let's note it as another machine in the area and keep our eyes out for infractions."

The council meeting concluded, and Hugh felt uneasy about the news he heard. There had been no indication that William at this point would be involved with any new business owner, but to be frank, he didn't even know much about what work he was doing.

Before going home, he downed a few friendly drinks with Stapleton at the bar. When he relaxed enough from the liquor to face home, he left to wander back to Eliza. Their daughter Margaret was walking now and into everything, and he could tell that Eliza looked overwhelmed by the household and his constant absence. Nothing changed in their relationship. She drifted away from him emotionally and he from her. Whatever he had seen in her when they married years ago faded into obscurity, only adding to the frustration of his life.

Chapter Twenty

THE GREATEST OF GIFTS

December 20, 1866

William scrimped and saved to purchase a used frock coat in good condition, along with a vest, trousers, and shirt for his wedding day. He determined to look as handsome as nature would allow alongside Mary as they took their vows. As he gazed at himself dressed and ready to meet her at the church, the surreal moment tasted both sweet and bitter.

With his brother in Australia, his mother in the grave, and his estrangement with Hugh, a familial loneliness stared back at him in the reflection. The family he once knew as a young boy had fractured and gone in different directions from the grave to another country. If things were different, he would have liked Hugh to stand by him as best man. John mentioned his encounter with his brother at the graveside, and Hugh's disinterest in his wedding pained him. Instead, Reggie Cooper would take that place, and he and his wife would be the needed witnesses for the ceremony.

Miss Beecham, of course, took care of Mary's needs for the past months and fussed over her like a mother. Without parents or siblings of her own to attend, she relied only on her uncle to be family to witness their joining.

With the banns now read and their private counseling with the vicar ended, William felt ready to take the next step in life. To his embarrassment, however, he had never been with a woman and the evening together as husband and wife would be a personal challenge. The only time he and Hugh ever spoke about what lay beneath a lady's skirt had been when his brother had a few too many drinks. The rude words associated with a woman's workings, as well as Hugh's abundant fascination with tits, as he called them, hadn't revealed anything of truth to William about what making love to a woman would be like.

He took out his old pocket watch, flipped the lid, and noted he was going to be late if he didn't stop his fantasy-filled expectations of the meaning of true womanhood. He hoped Mary wouldn't be appalled at his under muscular stature compared to other men when he bared his chest.

"You've got the brains," he said aloud, assuring himself the good Lord had given him the more precious portion. However, having both brains and brawn might have instilled in him more self-confidence.

The ceremony was not to be a large one as Mary and William agreed to a more private affair. Reggie Cooper and his wife and daughter would attend, along with Miss Beecham and Mrs. Goodson. Her uncle, of course, would perform the ceremony, and afterward, they would travel back in a carriage to the vicarage for a reception breakfast. Apparently, Mrs. Goodson involved a few other lady friends to help with the preparations.

By the time William arrived close to ten o'clock, his nerves were on edge. As soon as John saw him enter the side door, he grabbed him by the arm and led him out into the sanctuary.

"Where you been, William? You're late."

"Late?" He pulled out his watch and noted the time. When the vicar showed him his watch that indicated ten minutes of ten, his heart sank.

"Oh God, my watch is slow."

"Oh God, yes, and poor Mary cried, certain you had left her at the altar."

Mortified about what had happened, he nervously stood on the spot he should have been already. A wave of dizziness passed, and his palms sweat. It took him a moment to focus as he watched Miss Beecham walk down the aisle ahead of Mary. Finally his eyes shifted to Reggie, who looked as if he were on the verge of laughing at his predicament. His wife's facial expression remained somber, and their daughter sat wide-eyed next to her, staring at him.

Miss Beecham stepped off to the side, and then Mary came down the aisle alone. At that moment, he wished that her father were alive to escort his daughter.

Dressed in the most stunning dress of ivory silk he had ever seen, Mary glided toward him. She wore a matching wedding bonnet with flowers and frills, tied with a wide silk ribbon underneath her chin. A small bouquet of white roses were in her gloved hands. Miss Beecham beamed with pride, as she no doubt helped Mary with her choice of dress, which made her look like an angel.

When she joined him at the altar, he had never been as sure of a decision as he had at that moment. Even weeks before the wedding, he sensed that they were one in spirit.

"I'm sorry for being late," he whispered. "Blame my watch."

She looked at him with eyes of forgiveness. "Doesn't matter. You're here now."

"Shall we begin?" John cleared his throat and snickered.

"Please do," William replied.

"Dearly beloved, we are gathered together here in the sight of God and in the face of this congregation to join together this man and this woman in holy matrimony; which is an honorable estate, instituted of God in the time of man's innocence..."

William listened to the lengthy discourse that Mary's uncle read from the *Book of Common Prayer*. He paid attention and waited for the critical question of the ceremony.

"William Leighton, wilt thou have this woman to be thy wedded wife, to live together after God's ordinance in the holy estate of matrimony? Wilt thou love her, comfort her, honor and keep her, in sickness and in health; and, forsaking all others, keep thee only unto her, so long as ye both shall live?"

With no hesitation and a broad smile on his face, he responded, "I will."

"Mary Booker, wilt thou have this man to thy wedded husband, to live together after God's ordinance in the holy estate of matrimony? Wilt thou obey him and serve him, love, honor, and keep him, in sickness and in health; and, forsaking all others, keep thee only unto him, so long as ye both shall live?"

"Yes." She giggled. "I mean I will."

Her uncle snickered at her response and then continued with the ceremony. It seemed like an eternity until they finally reached the conclusion. When he pronounced them husband and wife, the elation in William's heart grew tenfold.

They signed the registry, held hands tightly, and gazed at each other with eyes that sparkled with joy.

"Congratulations, William," Reggie said, coming up and giving him his best wishes.

Miss Beecham hugged Mary tightly with tears in her eyes while her uncle beamed with pride. When everything ended, they returned to the vicarage for food, laughter, and well wishes. The day had been perfect in William's mind. The only taint upon it had been the absence of his brother.

The night was cold and dark when they returned to their home. Weeks before, William moved from his flat and rented an affordable terrace house off Fenney Street on the edge of Lower and Higher Broughton. It wasn't anything fancy by any means, but it was clean, comfortable, and the neighbors consisted of good working folk like himself. Plenty of children played in the streets.

William lit a fire in the small hearth in their bedroom and put candles around the room to lighten the interior. He hoped that his first sight of a woman's breast would be something worth seeing instead of groping for it under the covers.

"Hope you don't mind the candles. I got some extra for our special night," he said.

He already removed his frock coat and unbuttoned his white cotton shirt. His shoes were neatly placed by the chair near the door. Mary, still in her wedding dress, acted uneasy, fiddling with her hands.

"It's cold in here," she complained, walking to the windows and drawing the curtains shut.

"Come here by the fire, love, and get warm. Should heat up soon." He hoped it would be so hot she would want to take the dress off without having to coax her to do so. Already he figured he'd slip out of his cotton shirt and hoped she wouldn't be discomfited seeing his nakedness. William's chest wasn't as hairy as he would have liked it to be since his fair skin and lighter hair hadn't given him the dark looks that some women liked better.

Mary continued to fidget, so he came to her side by the fire and slipped his hand around her waist.

"Don't be nervous," he assured her in a low tone. "Are you afraid?"

She sucked in a quick breath. "Afraid? No, I'm not afraid. Miss Beecham told me everything I need to know."

William's brow rose above his right eye. "Is that a fact? I wished someone would have told me everything I needed to know."

Mary burst out in a giggle at his remark, and he flashed a roguish smirk. "Mary, you're my first. You married an unskilled man in the affairs of the flesh. Never been with a woman but tonight I will be."

He leaned over and kissed her on the cheek.

Apparently that wasn't enough, because Mary flung her arms around him and gave him a passionate kiss that showed courage rather than fear. Taken back by her aggressiveness, William looked at her in astonishment.

"I'm not shy about intimacy," Mary firmly said. Her nervous jitters passed, and the attractive, strong female he had married emerged. "Do you want to take off my dress? I want to take off your shirt," she teased, tugging on his sleeves.

"Yes, I want to take off your dress," William said. "Turn around and let me undo all those infernal buttons." His nimble fingers quickly released her bodice, and William parted the dress, revealing her back and upper shoulders. The perfect white complexion looked heavenly, and instinctively he kissed her skin. As he did so, Mary pulled her arms out of the bodice and dropped it on the floor. Without his help, she undid her skirt and stepped out, leaving her in her petticoat and crinoline hoop.

"Good Lord," he exclaimed. "So that's that contraption that billows your skirt?"

Mary laughed. "Well, yes, you've never seen one?"

"Can't say that I have," he replied.

Mary pulled the tie that held it in place around her waist and stepped out of it. "Best to keep it from the fireplace," she said. "I have read that a few ladies have gone up in flames because of them." She pushed it out of the way. "Now your shirt, please."

Obeying his wife's command, he slipped out of the cotton shirt. After baring himself before her, he struggled with his inadequacy that he hadn't the muscular display of a prizefighter. Regardless, her eyes glanced at him approvingly, which only gave him the courage to undress her completely. Mary helped as he unlaced her corset, and she eventually slipped out of her bloomers. When they dropped to the floor in front of him, he was astonished at the fine-looking form of a woman. Obviously he had seen pictures of naked women and stone statues here and there, but nothing did the female figure justice as it had at that moment only inches from his body. She was the most gorgeous creature he had ever seen. Mary saw the approval in his eyes.

"I'm not ashamed in front of you, William. I hope you find me pleasing."

He stepped toward her and gathered her into his arms. The fire that Hugh told him about ran through his veins. Even though he could barely breathe, he kissed Mary ardently. When he did so, she moaned, and between the two, the flames of passion ignited. There was nothing more to wait for now as he took her hand and led her to their bed.

A new chapter in his life had arrived.

Chapter Twenty~One

SENSATIONAL OUTRAGE

Hugh pulled up his collar and lowered the rim of his hat. "I've got a job tonight," he said to Eliza, as he stood by the door. He patted the pistol in his waistband that had been loaded with balls and ready to use if needed. Eliza remained silent, but her anger stared back at him through dark eyes.

"As a delegate now, I make more money. With me additional bricklaying jobs, Eliza, we can move away from the filth of the slums."

"Where would we go?"

"I don't know, but anything is better than this hellhole with another child on the way." Margaret stood by Eliza, hugging her skirt. He hadn't been the most attentive father to the young girl. Most times when he approached, she pulled away with fear in her eyes. Eliza poisoned her mind against him, and he admitted his drunken rages didn't help. When a boy came into the family, things would be different.

"Be careful," she said in a low tone.

He looked at her cautiously, knowing that she really didn't care what happened to him. "Don't worry 'bout me," he replied. "I can take care of meself."

Hugh opened the door and disappeared into the cold night to meet the lads for a few ales until the time was ripe for the attack. The Pack Horse Pub was crowded and smoky, thanks to those who came with Christmas cheer for the season. Naturally, Hugh hadn't an ounce of joy or regard for Christian holidays. Tonight though he decided to take part of his earnings and get Margaret and Eliza a small token gift for the season. Also, he planned to bring home a large fowl bird for her to cook for dinner. As far as a church service and the like, he refused to go and knew that Eliza despised going alone.

He ordered an ale and found Steve Brown at a corner table waiting for him. When he saw Hugh, he grinned and lifted his glass. "Might as well have a few. It's a damn cold night out there."

After sitting down, Hugh made a joke. "Well, we'll have a large fire to keep us warm, so I wouldn't worry about it." He glanced around. "The other lads joining us for a drink or meeting us there?"

"Dodson and his friend will meet us. They'll have the soaked shavings we can use and matches." Brown glanced at Hugh's midsection. "You got the other?"

Knowing he meant the pistol, he nodded his head rather than saying the words in case patrons eavesdropped on their conversation.

"I'm curious," Steve said after taking a slurp of his drink. "You heard from your brother?"

"Yeah, Aaron's letter finally arrived, and Pickett read it for me. He made the voyage safely, and I had Pickett write him back about Mam dying."

"That's not the brother I mean," Steve grimly replied. "You're avoiding the obvious."

Hugh glanced away at the crowd that sounded rowdier than they did when he arrived. Someone broke out in a Christmas carol, and others joined in song. It irritated him, and he gulped his glass ready for another.

"You going to answer me or not?" Steve pressured him.

"He got married or something—today I think. Can't remember."

"Shite, you're kidding me," he exclaimed. Steve broke out into a fit of laughter. "You didn't go, I take it?"

"I didn't get invited."

"Damn. I imagine he's fucking a woman at the same time while we're here at the pub." Steve chortled.

Hugh enjoyed the dig and joined in the jovial hilarity. Frankly, it created an amusing picture in his mind, wondering if William even knew what to do.

"He'll probably faint the first time he sees a tit." Hugh sputtered in laughter.

The two drank another ale, passing the hours until it was time to leave. Tonight would be an attack on a master brickmaker named Baker, whose business was out of the district. The company had been crossing lines with machine-made bricks, bringing them into the city. The union had clear rules regarding no out-of-district bricks for sale in Manchester.

The society didn't give a damn if another district purchased Manchester bricks for construction. Inside the boundary lines, though, masters were fools for not protecting their localities as far as Hugh was concerned. No one out of the district would bring in machine-made bricks on his watch. The attack tonight would be the second warning. They had previously given the company's carter a good beating and a stern caution when he tried to deliver bricks once before. Didn't do any good because the offenses continued.

The severity of tonight would result in an attack on the horses in his stables. As long as the business had no means of transporting bricks with horses and their carters were given a good wallop, the message would be clear—stay out of Manchester.

As the five of them congregated at the meeting location, Hugh inspected the area, taking note of the watchman at the gatehouse. No dogs were in sight, but if one attempted to attack him, his pistol would put a swift end to it.

The night, cold and dark, gave him a shiver in his thin frock coat. He could see his breath as he whispered to the crew.

"Okay, lads, you know the plan. No talking. Keep your heads down, and run like hell once the fire goes up."

Once again, they scaled the fence and crawled among the shadows until they made their way to the stables. Hugh told the men to wait in the dark and keep watch while he entered to check out the location. Four horses were in individual stalls along with a pony. Hugh noted a fine-looking mare among them, chestnut in color, who didn't like his presence. Her ears perked up, and her eyes widened when he put a rope around her neck and led her to the front of the stable. He tethered her in a narrow spot where she couldn't move, in clear sight where the owner could see her suffer.

After motioning to Dodson, he brought in the shavings they soaked in naphtha and placed them strategically in the stables. Hugh set the last handful on the ground under the belly of the mare, who started to make a ruckus by pulling on the rope and neighing.

"Light the others," Hugh instructed Dodson in a hasty voice. "I'll do her."

Dodson hastily did his worst, running from the ignited shavings and out the stable door. The mare kicked in fear, and Hugh rejected any remorse as he lit the flammable material that rapidly shot up and engulfed the horse in flames. By the time he ran from the barn, the watchman arrived, screaming at the top of his lungs.

"Fire! Police! Fire!"

The mare let out a shriek that Hugh never heard before, and the foolish watchman ran by him into the inferno to save the other horses. As the crew ran off into the dark, Brown halted to set fire to the carts, leaving little if anything for the owner to move his machine-made bricks.

They rounded the corner toward the street in a full run, and the whistle of a policeman blew behind him. He cursed under his breath, not expecting to see any patrols at this time in the morning.

When he glanced over his shoulder, the constable was in hot pursuit with ire in his eyes and determination that Hugh could not outrun. He pulled the pistol from his waistband, turned around, and fired a shot across the man's shoulder. It apparently did the trick, as the man ducked, giving Hugh time to increase the distance between them. He was about to turn and run down a dark alley, when two hands grabbed his coat collar, twisted him hard, and threw him to the ground. The remainder of his cohorts dispersed into the darkness and were free.

He looked up from the cold pavement to see a policeman's club coming down on his head, and he was able to deflect it with his arm. The club hit it hard, breaking the forearm bone. A crunching sound filled his ears, and Hugh screamed in pain.

"You fucking hooligan," the policeman screamed, wrestling the gun from his other hand. "I ought to burn you alive like you did that horse."

The other officer that he shot at grabbed him as well, hoisting him to his feet. His fist balled and hit Hugh in the jaw, knocking him down to the ground again. "That's for shooting at me, you bastard."

As he gazed up through blurry eyes at the two policemen, a kick lodged in his ribs. A god-awful pain burst inside his body. The club came whirling down toward his head again, and then everything went black.

The cold stone cell sent shivers down Hugh's spine as he regained consciousness. His eyes fluttered open, and pounding pain greeted him. After attempting to move, the throbbing in his arm, head, and ribs nearly drew him back into unconsciousness. It would have been a better state than the present.

"Hope the hell you rot in prison," a voice boomed, echoing off the stone walls.

Hugh glanced up, seeing a man stand there who

he recognized to be Baker.

"You sadistically killed my best mare, so I'm going to make damn sure you're thrown in prison for this atrocity, you bloody bastard."

"Dead is she? She squealed like a pig when she went up in flames," Hugh shot back, keeping the ire alive. He could taunt the man just as good. "It's your fault—not mine. You and your machine-made bricks taking the jobs of good men."

"The ignorance of your class is astounding," the man said, growling his words through his teeth. "You'll never stop the progress, and you can be damn sure we masters will band together to make sure we stop the likes of your kind. I know who you are, Leighton. You've made a name for yourself among the businessmen in Manchester and beyond. What will happen to your poor wife and child now? To the workhouse, I imagine, to rot there while you rot behind bars."

"I'll not be in prison. The union will protect me." Hugh huffed, climbing to his feet. The physical exertion exacerbated the agony, and he fell back down on the cold slab that was supposed to be a ledge to sleep on.

"See you in court." The man shook his head at him and then disappeared.

Groaning in agony, Hugh bellowed. "Guard, guard! I need medical attention!" He screamed for minutes until one showed up at the bars and peered at him.

"Shut up," he barked. "No surgeon for you. You can rot until tomorrow afternoon." He turned his back on him and walked away, leaving Hugh in misery.

The cell reeked of urine, and the cold stone walls sent tremors through his body. As he glanced around, he couldn't believe how things turned out. How in the hell did the police get there so fast? It was two o'clock in the morning, and they checked—no patrols were in the area at that time of night. It didn't make any sense. Perhaps Baker somehow knew that he had been on the target list and asked for the patrols in anticipation. If that was the case, it only meant one thing—a rat was in their midst. Someone had tipped him off, but who in the union would have the gall to risk their own life for some damn brickmaker?

He moved slightly, and the bone in his left arm floated to the side. It needed to be set, or he'd be deformed for sure, unable to work again. The idea sent him into a panic, and he climbed to his feet and came to the iron bars.

"I need help now!" His voice echoed down the corridor.

"You're off your chump if you think they be sending anyone," a man in the cell next to him yelled. "Shut your mouth and let the rest of us get some sleep."

The sound of other voices grumbled from the darkness, so he stumbled backward and sat down on the ledge. The cell walls closed in on Hugh as if he had been relegated to the dark corners of hell. Things had gone terribly wrong, and he feared the outcome for Eliza, his daughter, and unborn babe. The fleeting thought of finding William and reaching out for help came to mind, but he couldn't grovel to him now. Even though he was in the worst predicament of his life, he had to keep his head together and especially his pride.

Chapter Twenty-Two

CONSEQUENCES

The sensation of waking up next to a naked woman sent a rush of warmth through William's body the moment he realized Mary's breasts pressed against his back. She wrapped herself around his body like a blanket. Her legs were tucked next to his, and her arm slung around his waist. Married life had its pleasures, and his body responded in like manner.

Their joining for the first time the night before changed him inwardly. He had the makings of a real man now and could conquer the world with Mary at his side. The act of lovemaking had been more pleasurable than he anticipated. Though Mary experienced discomfort as virgin women do, she didn't appear to mind him at all. In fact, she groaned and moaned with unbridled vocals, which only encouraged him.

She stirred, and William rolled over. "Good morning, love," he whispered. His fingers pushed the strands of hair out of her eyes.

"Oh, let me sleep," she groaned.

"Sleep? Now why should I let you sleep?" he teased her, letting the palm of his hand slide up and down her naked frame. Her eyes shot open.

"Miss Beecham warned me about the mornings," she said, looking at him with a serious gaze.

"What does Miss Beecham know about such things? She's never been married." William scoffed at her remark.

"I cannot tell you how she knows lest I break a confidence."

"Oh, I see."

"The way you're stroking me, I dare say you're one of those men."

"One of what men?" William chortled.

"You want something."

"Perhaps I do," he said, flipping Mary and climbing on top of her. She smiled back at him as if she didn't mind at all his manly maneuver. After giving her an ardent kiss, she flung her arms around his neck. He would have taken it a step further, but suddenly a bang came at the front door downstairs. It startled both of them. William jolted and rolled off her body. When the knock came hard again, Mary shot up.

"Who is that?"

"Don't know," William replied. "Better find out."

He swung his legs over the edge of the bed, grabbed his trousers, and pulled them up. "Where's my shirt," he said, frantically looking through the discarded clothes on the floor as the banging continued.

"There, by the chair." Mary pointed to a ball of linen.

As he slipped his arms through the sleeves and hastily buttoned up, he looked at Mary and with alarm in his voice spoke. "You stay here."

She shook her head in agreement, as another pounding rattled the hinges. William ran down the stairs and peeked out the window to see Mason standing at the door. He flung it open, and Mason pushed indoors.

"Good God, man, it's freezing outside. What took you so long?"

William noted a light snowfall dust the ground.

"What the hell are you doing here at this hour?"

"Sorry to interrupt your marital bliss," he replied. "But there's been trouble at the union."

"What trouble that I need to hear about at this hour?" William ranted.

"It's your brother," Mason stated somberly. "Hugh went out on enforcement last night with other lads."

William's stomach knotted at the sound of his brother's name. Instantly the worst possible scenario came to mind—he was dead. "Is he…"

"No, no, but he got arrested last night. I guess the police who caught him gave him a good thrashing. He's in the Ashton-Under-Lyne jail."

"Good God," William moaned. He staggered to a chair. "What was he doing there?"

"Master brickmaker by the name of Baker had been transporting machine-made bricks into the Manchester district. The lads went to kill the horses."

"How many?"

"I believe Brown and Dodson went and a few others." Mason pulled up a chair by the table and sat down with William.

"How in the hell did you find out about it?"

"For the life of me, William, if I tell you how, you

cannot tell another soul or the union will kill me."

Knowing how far the union would go in some issues, William agreed. "Yes, of course."

"There's a mole on the enforcement council. He tipped off Baker that retribution was coming, so Baker asked the police to post extra patrols in anticipation."

William thrust his fingers through his hair and swore. "Damn," he exclaimed. "Why put his life on the line like that?"

"His daughter is engaged to Baker's son, that's why. He wanted to protect the family."

As he mulled over the news, William looked at Mason, who hadn't conveyed what damage, if any, they had done. "What did Hugh do?"

Mason shifted in his seat and shook his head. The look on his face displayed disgust as his lips spoke the words.

"Hugh and his cohorts set the stables on fire. Except Hugh took Baker's best mare, tied her to a post, and then lit shavings underneath her belly that had been soaked to ignite. The poor animal went up in a ball of flames."

William thrust his head in the palm of his hands and moaned. "Oh my God. What the hell is wrong with him?"

"William?" Mary's voice called from the top of the stairs. "Is everything all right?"

He stood to his feet and looked up at her. "Yes, fine, love. Just a friend from the union with some news. Go back to bed. I'll tell you later."

"All right." She turned around and retreated into the bedroom.

"Sorry to intrude on your honeymoon, William, but I knew you'd want to be informed."

"No apology necessary," he said, returning to the chair. He thought for a moment. "I don't suppose Hugh will want to see me."

"Don't suppose he will. My advice is to let it play out and see what the charges will be. No doubt the union will hire the attorney to represent him."

"No doubt," William concurred.

"What of Eliza? Has anyone told her?"

"I don't know," Mason said. "I suppose eventually they will."

"Good Lord, what a mess," William moaned. "I should see her straightaway at least and make sure she's taken care of in the meantime."

Mason rose to his feet. "I'll let you get back to your new wife," he said. "Sorry about your brother, William."

"Well, thanks for coming." He shook Mason's hand. After he opened the door, the snowflakes fell like white cotton fluff from the sky. "Best get home as soon as you can. Looks like we're in for some snow."

"Take care."

William nodded in return and then closed the door behind him. Perhaps he should have been surprised at the outcome, but he always had a gut inkling something like this would happen. The union violence had gotten out of control, and the targeting of brickmakers with machines troubled him.

He climbed the stairs and opened the door of their bedroom to see Mary sitting up in bed. Her knees gathered toward her chest, and her face etched with concern.

"What happened?"

William crawled into bed next to her and put his arm around her shoulder. "My brother got arrested last night for an attack."

"Oh, goodness. What did he do?"

"Love, you don't want to hear the horror of it. Frankly, I can't get the image out of my mind."

"William, I'm sorry."

"Eliza doesn't know. We should go see her this afternoon if that's all right with you. I need to check on her welfare and that of Margaret."

"Yes, of course."

"It's snowing outside," William remarked.

"It is!" Mary threw back the cover and jumped out of bed stark naked. When she reached the window, she spread the curtains and squealed like a little girl. "It's gorgeous." She gasped. "Big white flakes!"

"Well, you can go play in it later, if you wish." William got out of bed and came behind her body. He pressed himself against her and enjoyed the warmth of her smooth skin. "Come back to bed, wife," he enticed her, kissing her on the neck.

Mary slowly turned around and gazed at him as she encountered his bulging need pressing against her body.

"It's the morning engagement Miss Beecham spoke about." She giggled. "All right, husband, as long as you are gentle."

"Gentle it is," William said, taking her hand and leading her back to bed.

The squall of snow passed within the hour, and

the sun parted the clouds, illuminating the landscape in brilliant white. William paid a carriage to take them to Hugh's residence. He hadn't been there since the row they had months before. No quarrel had come between him and Eliza, and he hoped for a welcome. He knocked on the door, and a moment later it flung open to reveal Dodson on the other side. William sucked in a breath, bracing for the worst.

"What are you doing here, Leighton?" he asked, scowling at him. Brown came up behind him, flashing his dark eyes and displeasure.

"I'm here to see Eliza," he announced, standing his ground.

"William!" Eliza's voice boomed from behind the men, and she pushed them aside. "Let him in," she insisted.

Grasping Mary's hand tightly, William pushed past the men and entered indoors. The chill from outside hung in the air. No coals were in the hearth, and his brows scrunched together in concern. Eliza gave him a frantic hug as tears streamed down her cheeks.

"What am I to do, William? What am I to do?"

When she pulled away, he noted her rounded belly. She carried another child, and William's heart sank. Poor Margaret stood in the corner shivering, and Mary instinctively went to her and gathered her in her arms.

"We are taking care of things," Dodson announced. "I've told Eliza here that the union will watch out for her."

"Then why are you standing here doing nothing? There's no coal in the hearth, it's freezing in here, and she needs help now."

A sour expression contorted Dodson's face, and Brown interjected. "We'll take care of it," he growled. "We just got here and told Hugh's wife he's incarcerated."

Eliza pulled her shawl tight around her shoulders. William, angry at the affair, pulled out a handful of shillings from his pocket and gave it to Dodson.

"Go get her some coal now," he ordered. "You," he shouted at Brown. "Buy her some meat and bread. If the union is supposed to care for her, it can't wait any longer."

William stomped to the door, opened it wide, and pointed outside. "Get the hell out and don't come back until you've provided for this woman."

"I'm doing this for Hugh," Dodson spat, stomping toward the door. "Not for you."

"Then do it!"

The men left, and William shoved the door shut with a bang.

"Do you have any wood, Eliza, any coal at all?"

"No. Hugh was supposed to bring some back last night. Our last burned out hours ago, and when he didn't return, I didn't know what to do," she wailed aloud hysterically. William gathered her in his arms.

"We'll take care of you and Margaret." He pulled away and looked at her belly. "Didn't realize you were expecting."

"Aye, the baby is due in March," she blubbered. "What will happen if Hugh is in prison?" Her fingers clutched his forearms tightly. "Oh, William, I don't wanna to go to the workhouse. I'll just die there. I know it."

Mary glanced at him forlornly, holding Margaret in her arms to keep her warm. She sat in the rocking chair with the child in her lap, attempting to comfort her as well.

"The union will hire an attorney," William said. "They'll do their best to get him off."

"What did he do this time?" Eliza asked with pleading eyes.

"You don't need to hear the particulars. No need to talk of it in front of Margaret either."

"It's something terrible, isn't it? He's been drinking, angry, yelling, and…"

"Has he hit you again?"

"Sometimes he slaps me across the cheek," she answered. "Mostly me fault 'cause I can't control me tongue."

"Oh, Eliza," Mary moaned.

Mary handed Margaret to William, and he took the toddler into his arms. The unfortunate girl shivered in his embrace. His wife hugged Margaret, whispering encouraging words in her ears. Mary's empathy surrounded his sister-in-law like a warm blanket.

"This is my wife, Mary, by the way," William announced. "We got married yesterday."

"Married?" Eliza said, wiping her nose with her sleeve. She mumbled congratulations.

"Finally did it," William said.

"I'm so happy for you," Eliza said with tears still streaming down her cheeks.

Proud of his wife and intent on looking out for Eliza's welfare, they stayed until Dodson and Brown returned with supplies.

William quickly grabbed the coal and went to the stove to start a fire. Brown gave the food to Eliza, which she gratefully received. When warmth returned to the dreary room, William stood to his feet and faced the others.

"Are they allowing visitors at the jail?" William inquired.

"Don't think your brother would care to see you," Brown said plainly.

"Probably not, but it's about time." William pondered in silence, struggling with his mixed emotions about his wayward sibling. Though the visit would be unpleasant, a compelling force inwardly urged him to go as he may not see Hugh again for some time.

"Mary, will you stay here with Eliza until I return?"

"Yes, of course. Do what you must," she replied in an understanding tone. Filled with sympathy for others and supportive of his decisions, William gazed at her lovingly.

"You two want to come with me?" He looked pointedly at Dodson and Brown.

"Guess it can't hurt," Brown said.

After giving a thankful kiss on Mary's cheek, he left with the two men.

Chapter Twenty-Three

THE VISIT

Around noon, Hugh had been dragged off to the infirmary and to a butcher of a surgeon that set his arm. He acted as if his low class deserved every bit of pain that he inflicted upon him. With one hard jerk, he pulled his arm straight, causing Hugh to yelp in agony.

"You're fortunate it's a clean break. Otherwise, I would have had to cut your arm off," he informed him with little emotional compassion.

"Can't you give me anything for the pain?" Hugh moaned.

"The jail doesn't waste its money on laudanum for prisoners. You'll have to grit your teeth and bear through it."

He watched as he placed two splintered boards against his skin and tied them firm by winding cloth around them until tight. It appeared the jail didn't care one bit about the health of its prisoners, and Hugh feared his arm would never be the same.

"Five to six weeks," the surgeon announced. "Should be mended by then. Can't say it will work as good as before." He chortled a laugh.

"You fucking bastard," Hugh spat.

"Watch your mouth, or I can have you flogged for

that remark," the surgeon replied, flashing a dark glance.

Hugh shut his lips and was soon dragged by the other arm back to his cell, groaning at every push and pull along the way. The jailer opened the bars, threw him inside, and he landed on his sore rib cage. If the guards didn't kill him, he'd soon die from the pain. As the metal door slammed shut, the sound of the key turning and the lock setting echoed off the walls. He had been caged like an animal.

"There's some food there for you," the guard said, nodding toward a bowl on the stone ledge. "The best fiddles in town." He laughed, walking away.

Hungry as hell, Hugh picked up the plate and sniffed the contents. It smelled like rotten meat ground up with grain, and he feared to eat it. The odor wafted up his nose, nauseating his stomach.

"I'd rather starve," he roared, throwing it against the wall. "I'd rather starve!" Angry, he sat back down on the ledge and held his throbbing arm. It would have been a good time to wail like a baby and cry about it, but instead, he just gritted his teeth at the pounding discomfort.

A few minutes later, the jailer approached his cell. "You got visitors," he said.

Hugh glanced up and saw Brown and Dodson on the other side of the bars. "What took you so long?" He rose to his feet and faced them. "You getting me out of here?"

"Shite, Hugh, they did rough you over good," Brown said, eying his injuries with a grimace.

"Broken arm, broken ribs, and a damn knot on me head from a club," he said, rubbing it with the palm of his hand. I'd laugh about it if I could, but it would hurt."

"Sorry for the troubles," Dodson said. "We were long gone by the time they caught you. I think they knew we were coming."

"I surmised as much," Hugh remarked. "We have a snitch among us." He paused. "Did the horses all die?"

"From what I hear the mare got the worst of it. The watchman got two horses out of the stables. The others died."

"Good. The carts gone?"

"Burned to a crisp," Dodson answered.

"Well, we accomplished what we set out," Hugh remarked with a satisfied grin on his face.

"The union will be sending a barrister tomorrow to talk to you about your defense," Brown said.

"Do you know what the charges are yet? Nobody says nothing to me here."

"Not yet," Brown said. "I'm assuming destruction of property."

"Hope not attempted murder. I shot at that officer but made sure to miss. Didn't want murder on me hands."

"Someone else came with us, Hugh," Brown announced. He glanced nervously over his shoulder. "William is here."

"What the hell did you bring him for?" Hugh growled under his breath. His heart pounded in his throat. "I don't want to see him."

"I guess you don't have a choice since I'm out here and you're in there. Not like you can walk away from it," William announced, coming out of the shadows.

"Boys, give us a minute," he asked, nodding at them to retreat.

Dodson and Brown withdrew, leaving him face-to-face with his brother. A snide remark came to mind, and without forethought, Hugh spoke it in hopes it would dissuade William from staying.

"Did you enjoy your new wife's cunt last night?" he snarled. "I thought about your wedding night, wondering if you knew how to find your way inside." He half expected William to reach through the bars with his bare hands and strangle him. Instead, he just stood there with a blank look on his face apparently unmoved by his remark. "Good fuck was it?" Hugh probed again like a poker.

William shook his head back and forth and lowered his eyes. "Let me articulate it in the language you understand. You're such a zounderkite! A bumbling idiot! A fucking fool!"

"So what if I am?" he answered indifferently. The cold disregard remained in his eyes. "I told you I do what I do to protect the union men."

"You do what you do as an outlet to the drunken anger you carry around like a badge of honor or something. God, Hugh, you're ruining your life, your wife's and daughter's, and now a newborn baby on the way? Can't you live a decent life for their sake at least?"

"Oh, here we go again. Me windy-wallet brother, boasting about the moral high road he expects me to take along his side." He approached the bars and got face-to-face with William. "I'm not you. I don't want to be like you— I hate you and everything you stand for—your religion, your conservative politics, your plea for peace." He brought up phlegm from his throat and spat it at William's feet. "That's what I think of your values."

"You think anyone will want to hire you after you get out of jail? You'll be blacklisted by every master brickmaker and contractor in Manchester. You'd be better off in another country to find a new start after prison."

Hugh's stretched his arms through the bars and attempted to grab William, but he stepped back out of reach. Brown interjected.

"All right, enough of that," he said, pushing William aside. "It's best you be going now while we talk to Hugh about matters."

"Like I said last time," Hugh bellowed. "Get out."

William disappeared into the shadows, and Brown watched him as he withdrew. "He's gone," he said, assuring Hugh.

"Good."

"We best be going too," Dodson said. "Tomorrow, like we said, someone will be by to let you know what's happening. We'll get a good barrister, Hugh, to represent you in court."

"Why do I have the gut sense I'm doomed." He grunted. Hugh knew that the outcome would not go well for him, especially after Baker's threats. "Do me a favor. Take care of Eliza whatever happens. Promise me that much. I got a baby on the way," he desperately pleaded.

"Don't worry about it," Dodson assured him. "We've already stopped by and taken care of matters."

"Your brother will look in on her too," Brown remarked.

"I don't want his charity," Hugh snarled. "Don't want to be indebted to him for a bloody thing. You lads promise me you'll take care of her."

"Yeah, sure, sure," Dodson replied. "Don't worry."

A few hours later, William returned to Hugh's residence. Mary greeted him at the door, and he entered into a much warmer interior than he had found before.

"How'd it go?" Mary asked.

"As expected. He didn't want me there," William replied. He wasn't going to give her the entire gist of the conversation or his brother's crass remarks that burned in his mind like fire. When Hugh spat the words, he knew it was to rile him up, but William refused to react to his depravity.

"Oh, William, is he all right?" Eliza inquired.

"He's fine. A bit beat up from what I can tell. The police broke his arm with a club when they arrested him, but it's been set."

Eliza brought her hands to her mouth and gasped. "Oh dear Lord."

"He has bigger problems than a broken arm, I'm afraid." William spoke of the possible outcome. "The union's representative is meeting with him in the morning, but we don't know the charges yet."

"He's going to prison, isn't he?" Eliza questioned in a shaky voice. "I told him time and time again to stop what he was doing, but he wouldn't listen."

"It's not your fault," William said, reaching out and patting her hand. "Hugh's stubborn as hell and always has been. He's got a mind of his own, and no one can tell him what to do or think." His eyes shifted to Mary. "Unfortunately, he's paying for the poor decisions he's made in life. I hope to God that the outcome turns him around."

Eliza broke out into uncontrollable tears again, and William worried about her welfare. The union had better look out for her, or there'd be hell to pay from his hand.

"I'm going to give you my address, Eliza. If you need anything, you come to see me or send word. Do you promise you'll do that for Margaret's and the baby's sake?"

She nodded her head affirmatively while sniffing. Feeling emotionally exhausted, he glanced at Mary, who looked equally distraught about the day's events.

"We better get home," he said. "Looks like snow again."

They stood to their feet, and Eliza reached out and grabbed William's hand to give it a good squeeze. "Thank you."

William shoved his hand in his pocket and grabbed a few shillings, placing them in Eliza's palm. "You take this for now, and let me know if you need more."

She glanced at the amount and spoke in a shaky voice. "Thank you, William."

"I have no issue against you, Eliza, never had. You're a good woman—more than Hugh deserves, frankly." He smiled warmly at her. "Take care of yourself, Margaret, and that babe. You think it a boy or a girl?"

"Oh, boy, I hope. Hugh so wants a boy. For his sake, I hope it's a boy."

"Well, maybe a boy would be a good thing for him, right?"

Eliza shook her head.

After giving her a goodbye hug, William and Mary stepped out into the cold late afternoon. The clouds had returned, and the smell of moisture filled their nostrils.

"It's going to snow," Mary said. "Can smell it coming."

"Me too." William took her arm and wrapped it around his. "Let's go home and start a fire of our own."

"Will Hugh go to jail?" Mary asked.

"Probably so." William sighed in grief. "Be a miracle if they get him off."

"Like you said, maybe this will turn him around."

"Hope so. Don't know much else to do. New job starts next week. You're going back to the hat shop you love to work at. We have to focus on our lives, Mary. Hugh has made his choices, now he must live with them."

He tugged Mary closer and tried his best to push aside the bitter disappointment at the outcome of his brother's decisions. It was hard to understand how two people born of the same parents were so different from one another in values and thoughts.

The oddity of it all made him wonder about his children that Mary and he would bring into the world. Would they get along as siblings? Would one be good, the other evil, and other cursed with no ambition? The thought ran through him like the chill of the day. He hoped that the good Lord would see fit to give him good sons and daughters and likewise endow him with the wisdom to be a decent parent.

Chapter Twenty-Four

A New Beginning

January arrived, and William reported to Cooper's new location as agreed. With the machinery delivered and installation underway, William was excited to see the display of the invention.

The developments of the century excited William, and now that he had the chance to examine the machinery firsthand, he felt eager to do so. The only obstacle had been the union's continued rejection of progress. To face the opposition, William saw opportunities for master brickmakers to stand together and eventually convince ignorant members of the necessity of invention.

"William, over here," Reggie called after him. "I'm overwhelmed by progress." He pointed at the machine. "Look at it! It's a wonder."

"Indeed, but we need to get the right mixture to fill it with," he replied. "One thing at a time."

"I'm like a child with a new toy," Reggie confessed. His facial expression changed. "We must talk though."

Talk. He knew already what the discussion would entail, and he sucked in a breath to say the words before Reggie did. "About my brother, no doubt."

"Come into the office, William, and let's have a chat." A dread filled William's gut as he followed his employer behind closed doors. Reggie had made his mark with an office, ledgers on the side of his desk, and plenty of ideas in his brain. William wanted to be part of the building of his business, and at that moment, he feared it might come tumbling down around him like a wall of bricks.

He closed the door behind him but remained standing as Reggie took a seat behind his desk. "Is this about my brother?" Williams's voice trembled, but he kept his facial expression somber.

"I've heard that he's standing trial for the outrage at Baker's yard. Do you know the charges?

"Maliciously killing a horse—that's all I know," William responded, lowering his head.

"It's a grievous thing indeed what happened, and I'm sorry for the anguish he has caused Baker, you, and your family."

Surprised at the comment, his fear of reprisal lifted. "Thank you."

"When's the trial?"

"Mid-January, I believe."

"All right then, take your mind off of it. Have a seat and let's go over the next bit of business."

William sat down while Reggie shuffled some papers on his desk. "I took the liberty of putting advertisements in the *Manchester Courier* for men to operate the machine. We'll need five, to begin with, plus a crew for the field and men for the kiln. That's our first order of business."

"Agreed," William responded, leaning forward to pay attention.

"I've asked interested parties to come here at our location at ten o'clock this morning. Your first day's work is cut out for you with meeting the men that show up for employment."

Reggie had shown initiative that William liked. Ready for the challenge of being a foreman, William's excitement rose to new heights.

"You can use the office here to talk to the men individually." He thought for a moment. "Do we hire union or nonunion men? Go over the rules with me, William. Are we in the Manchester district or out?"

"We're in the district if you count the miles from the Royal Exchange. We'll need to hire union men."

"Well, we've discussed the wages between us already for the various positions, so I give you free rein to offer the men work." Reggie shoved some of the papers into his leather satchel and grabbed his hat. "I'm off on business elsewhere meeting with a contractor who has an upcoming job for a church in Bolton. The contractor needs bricks." A glint of determination shone in his eyes. "Since you have the art of persuasion in your voice, I can already see you in the years ahead procuring work for us rather than being a foreman. You have a good head on your shoulders, and I intend to use it to the fullest."

William gawked at Reggie in disbelief. "Your confidence in me is overwhelming, sir. Nevertheless, you have my word I intend to do my best while in your employ."

"Good!" Reggie rose to his feet and looked at the machine. "Why don't you go out there and talk to the men installing that contraption and find out more about how it works. I may have a business head for other matters, but when it comes to moving parts, I'm a bit daft." He laughed aloud.

An eagerness took over William's step as he went out toward the machine, eyeing it with interest. Reggie departed. The trust that he showed in his abilities gave him confidence for his first day on the job.

Suddenly the words "slave to none" floated through his thoughts. Only this time he didn't feel like a slave serving a master. Something had changed, and opportunities were opening up to him in a floodgate of blessings. Naturally, there would be obstacles ahead to overcome, most of which would be the union's continual fight against machinery. William had ideas, though, about master brickmakers forming their own consortium of sorts where they could protect one another and advocate for change. Eventually the union would have to come around.

"How does it work?" William asked one of the men.

"It's fairly simple," he replied. "Don't let the size of it or all the mechanical parts concern you. It works like a charm, albeit it's a bit noisy when the engine starts up to turn the gears."

For the next few minutes, William listened intently, taking in the information he needed. The man handed him a printed pamphlet from the company that further explained the mechanisms of the machine. He read how the parts worked together to take the clay mixture and form the bricks. It was an ingenious feat of engineering.

As the hour slipped by, men looking for work arrived. Astonished that he, after all these years, now could wear the hat of a foreman, he swore to himself that he would be fair in his dealings. He would not be like others who acted like angry bulls on the job sites. William had enough experience under his belt to know that workers wanted one thing above the shillings in their pockets—respect.

"I'm the foreman," he said, introducing himself to two gents who had arrived. "Are you're here to inquire about work?"

"Aye, sir," one lad nodded. "I'm Tom Nelson, and this here is Bob Pritchard."

"All right then," William replied. "Have either of you ever worked on a brickmaking machine?"

"I did at Browers's," Pritchard remarked. "Union drove him out of business."

Tom remarked, "I haven't, but Pritchard here tells me there's not much to running them."

"Pritchard, why don't you come with me in the office so we can talk?" He nodded at Tom. "You can look at the machine and tell me what you think. I'll speak with you in a few minutes."

William led Pritchard into the office and closed the door. He was a foreman now and proud of it.

After walking through the door of his new home life, William's nostrils immediately smelled dinner. Whatever Mary had cooked would be a welcome reprieve from a long day. Famished for food, he smiled at the sight of her dressed in an apron and stirring a pot on the iron cast stove. She swung around with a spoon in her hand and grinned.

"You're home."

"I am," he said, taking off his hat and throwing it on the chair. She narrowed her eyes at him.

"Please don't tell me that you are a sloppy person, William. You know very well there's a hook by the door, and that's where your hat and coat belong." She shook the spoon at him. "You might as well learn that I like order, and I intend to keep our home as such."

Put in his place, he grabbed the hat and found the hook. He slipped off his frock coat and hung it up as well, making sure it draped neatly in place.

"Is that better?"

"Much."

"What's for dinner? Smells delicious."

"Mutton stew," she announced, returning to stir the pot.

"Does my wife like to cook?"

"I do. My father always had a cook in the household to make meals, but I liked to watch and learn."

"I should be thankful," William said, realizing how little he knew about his Mary in many aspects.

"It will be ready soon, William. Sit down and tell me about your first day with Mr. Cooper. Is he a fair man? Do you get along?"

"Yes, he's a reasonable gentleman," William replied, pulling out a chair at the table and taking a seat. "The day went well. The machine arrived and has been installed, and I hired some men too."

"You did?" Mary's face beamed with interest. "You must tell me how it feels to be in that position."

"Mr. Cooper gave me the authority to start hiring a crew, which I attended to for some time during the day. He had placed an advertisement in the newspaper, and quite a few men arrived looking for work, as well as a couple boys."

Mary's attentiveness warmed his heart as she expressed interest in his affairs. Although she asked many questions, William eagerly answered each one.

"And how about you? Did you work at the shop today?"

"Yes, for a few hours," Mary replied with less enthusiasm than he had.

"Do you not care for it any longer?" He reached across the table and took her hand in his. "I want you to be happy, Mary."

"To be truthful, I am having second thoughts. Since we wed, my heart seems to be here at home. As my uncle said, perhaps some women are called to be homemakers and mothers rather than business savvy like men."

Taken back by her comment, he leaned in his chair and looked at her curiously. He hadn't expected such a quick change of heart, but he admitted as he glanced around the room, Mary had started to put her female mark upon the interior in subtle ways. Perhaps soon she would conceive, and the thought excited him.

"What about babies?"

"What about babies?" She swiftly repeated.

"Do you look forward to having our children?"

"That's a silly question, William." She scoffed at him. "If our activities in bed continue as they have been, I'll be with a child soon." She tilted her head and studied him for a moment. "Are you ready to be a father?"

"I'll have nine months to prepare for it, I suppose,

when the time comes." He glanced at the pot. "God, woman, I'm famished. Is it ready to eat?"

Mary laughed hysterically and bowed at the waist.

"What is so funny?" he queried.

"Slave to none." She chortled. "Your favorite phrase. I suppose I shall be your slave now."

"Never," he exclaimed, standing up and pulling her into his arms. "We are companions, love. Side by side on a quest for a better life."

"You're such a dreamer," she whispered, tracing her index finger across his lips. "That's what I love about you the most." Mary kissed him, and William enjoyed the before-dinner temptation in his arms.

Chapter Twenty-Five

An Untimely End

The bars to his cell opened, and the jailer looked at him with a scowl. They treated prisoners like the scum, and frankly, Hugh felt like it.

"You have a visitor," he announced.

A stout man with gray hair came into his lockup, carrying papers in his hand. "I'm your barrister, Mr. Biggs," he announced. "The union has hired me to represent you in court."

"I thought they had abandoned me," Hugh remarked, having heard nothing for days.

"I'll make this quick, Mr. Leighton."

Hugh stood before the well-dressed man, waiting for information.

"The prosecution will be lenient with you on the charges that are pending—"

"What are the charges?" He gruffly interrupted. "No one has told me a thing."

"Feloniously and maliciously killing a horse."

He wasn't sure the meaning of the first word but understood the second.

"As I was saying," Mr. Biggs continued. "The prosecution will go easy on you if you agree to give them the names of the others involved in the outrage at Baker's brickyard—namely all the men who accompanied you with the intent and purpose of doing harm to his property. Obviously others were involved in the arson of the stables and carts."

"You want me to snitch?" Hugh balked. He scowled in protest. "You cannot be serious, man. I'm not about to get me throat slit when I get out of jail for betraying union members I consider me friends. It's a death sentence."

"Is that your final answer, Mr. Leighton?"

"Aye," he said, standing firmly in place. "Have 'em charge me with the horse killing. I wasn't the one who set fire to the building or carts. Don't wanna go down for those offenses."

"Well, I'm afraid you may if you don't give up the names of those whom you are protecting."

"You're me barrister, dammit. Make sure I don't go down for the other charges," Hugh growled.

"Well, conceivably if you pled guilty to the killing of the horse, the judge may consider a more lenient sentence. We may be able to play on his sympathy since you have a child on the way."

Hugh thought for a moment. He didn't want to go to trial. What evidence did they have against him, other than grabbing him by the collar in a dark alley? Unless they could prove he did the damage, he wondered if he should fight it. Maybe he could get the lads he was protecting to agree to testify that he was somewhere else rather than torching a horse.

"Do I have any chance of winning in a trial? What evidence do they got against me?"

"A witness, I'm afraid, who can clearly identify you as the perpetrator of the crime."

"A witness?"

"Yes, the watchman recognized you as he ran by you into the stables to save the other horses."

"Damn," he spat.

"Mr. Leighton, if you will not give up the names of the other men, then my advice to you is to plead guilty to killing the horse. I'll approach the prosecution and see what, if anything, I can do."

"Fine," Hugh replied. He wanted to punch the wall for the damnable predicament he suffered because of the enforcement. Never once did he think he'd be caught during his participation. He had been too smart. If throats would be slit, surely the rat who tipped off the police they were coming deserved the edge of a knife.

The man called for the guard, who returned to let him out of the cell. When the door opened, Hugh wished he could flee between them and never return to the hellhole that he lived in for weeks. When they transferred him to prison, the thought chilled him to the bone. He had heard horror stories about life behind bars. Away from Eliza, Margaret, and a baby soon due, he feared for their well-being. Dodson and Brown hadn't been back to give him further assurance that the union would watch out for them in the meantime. The painful gnawing of worry wrenched his gut.

Steel bars met the locking mechanism with a clank, and the guard turned the key. Hugh sat down and put his head in his hands. In a few more days, he would know his fate.

The judge sat behind the bench in his scarlet

robe, with his head covered in a white wig. Hugh looked at his barrister, dressed in a black gown, who wore a wig as well. As far as his appearance, he stood in the accused box, in the same clothes he had worn the night of the raid at Baker's yard. He smelled like a pig, with his hair in disarray and his dirty face covered in a beard. Soon he'd be wearing prison garb. Having never been inside a courtroom, he remained like a statue, immovable, in one spot, frozen in trepidation. His hands were bound in chains, and a guard stood by his side with a nightstick he kept tapping in his palm.

"Mr. Leighton." The judge's deep voice reverberated off the dark wood panel walls of the chamber. "You have entered a plea of guilty for feloniously and maliciously killing a horse." His eyes focused on Hugh and narrowed. "You are not the first union member to stand before this bench that has been accused of the despotic nature of your class. The Manchester brick unions commit social tyranny far too often, in my opinion, lording their rules and edicts upon good citizens, whether they be fair or not. Mr. Baker here wanted nothing more than to maintain a business and earn an income like yourself."

Hugh glanced upward into the balcony at Baker, who leaned over the railing, watching the proceedings, and slowly returned his gaze to the judge.

"Your barrister here, Mr. Biggs, thinks that I should show you leniency for your participation because you have a young child to feed and a baby on the way." The judge pursed his lips together and folded his hands, laying them on top of the bench. "I, on the other hand, believe that you should have considered the consequences of your actions before your participation in this outrage and cruel act of burning a horse alive." He shook his head back and forth. "I cannot, for the life of me, understand the depravity of your mind to do such a heinously wicked wrong to an innocent animal." The judge sucked in a breath. "I'm of the opinion it's about time the court makes an example out of hooligan unionists like yourself to deter others in your class from participating in further outrages. I, therefore, sentence you to one year in prison."

The heart that thumped in Hugh's chest skipped a beat, and the air he held in his lungs expelled. He swore that the judge's words had wrapped around his neck, choking him to the point he could not breathe. He glanced up at Baker, who nodded at him in triumph, smirking at the sentence handed down.

"Guard, escort the prisoner to his new lodgings," the judge instructed.

His barrister ignored him completely, picked up the papers in front of him, said nothing further, and left the courtroom without a glance backward.

No one had come to his sentencing. Dodson and Brown were absent and no other union members arrived. A part of him wondered if William would appear to support him in some manner. His nonattendance suddenly made him angry regardless of the fact Hugh had pushed him away. Thankfully, Eliza stayed away, or she would have wailed at her predicament because of his foolhardiness.

"Come on you," the guard said, grabbing him hard by the arm and digging in his fingers.

He sneered in Hugh's face as if he could sense

through his fingertips the cold fear that ran through his veins. As he shoved him down the stairs from where he came, they roughly led him down a hallway. Another guard stood waiting with chains in hands. Hugh halted while the man knelt down and wrapped shackles around his ankles, causing him to shudder uncontrollably as they bound him for transportation.

Another push out the door and he came face-to-face with a prisoner transportation carriage.

"Where are you taking me?" he asked while climbing inside the box.

"New Bailey Prison, Salford." The guard looked at him. "It's no hotel, that's for sure. It's a real hellhole." He snorted. The guard slammed the door shut and latched it from the outside, locking him securely in the dark cage. After banging on the side, the carriage lurched forward as the horse pulled him to his destination.

Remorse for what he had done poured over his hardened heart. The thoughts of that night at Baker's stables flooded his mind. He remembered the mare's frightened look when he tethered her, knelt down, and piled the soaked shavings beneath her belly. When he lit the match and the wood ignited, he jumped to his feet and gawked at the flames shooting up her underside. She bolted, pulled on the rope, kicked, and wailed. By then Hugh had run out of the barn but looked over his shoulder to see her engulfed in the fires of hell.

Hugh rubbed his eyes with his fist, wanting the images to go away. The remorse for shooting the watchman with a gun had been nothing compared to the regret that choked him for killing the horse. He wondered as the carriage rolled ahead if it were merely the circumstances bringing about his sorry state of mind. Would he still give a damn if he were a free man? He couldn't say.

Hugh peeked out between the bars and saw people staring at the carriage traversing the crowded streets. If their disgusted looks weren't enough, he swore that the eyes of every horse that passed him on the way appeared wide-eyed at him in anger, neighing the words in his ears. "You got what you deserved."

The carriage arrived at its destination, slowed, and stopped inside a gated area. The doors opened, and Hugh was pulled by the collar out onto the cobblestone ground. It took a minute for his eyes to adjust from the darkness to the light, and when it finally did, the stone fortress loomed high above his head.

"Welcome to your new home," the guard said, pushing him toward the door. "Hard labor, gruel, and a cell so small you'll have to sleep like a baby with your legs tucked under your ass." Another guard opened a metal door, and Hugh halted his step, trembling.

"Not so tough now, are you unionist?" the guard taunted. With another push from behind, the shackles on his feet rattled, and he stumbled forward. Hugh swore that hell had opened and swallowed him whole. When he heard the bang of the door behind him and the jailer jingle keys, the cold reality of his situation sent waves of nausea through his belly. The next year of his life would be a horrific trial of endurance. It would either make him or break him, and he feared the latter would occur.

Chapter Twenty-Six

The Prodigal

Manchester, January 1867

As William sat at the table by himself, having a morning cup of tea, he reflected upon the past year with a mixture of emotions. Mary had chosen the red rose pattern. He recalled how odd it had been over a year ago to hold china between his fingers. Now after a prosperous year with Mr. Cooper, they had a set of bone china to call their own with plates, cups, saucers, and a teapot. To be honest, he wasn't that enthralled with the flowery design, but he would do anything to make Mary happy by surrounding her with lovely household items.

The brickmaking business had struggled to get off the ground after an unusually harsh winter, but Reggie's unrelenting ability to drum up business outside the district had kept them afloat. Strange as the apparatus looked, it continued to spew out thousands of preformed bricks in a fraction of the time than it took to produce by hand. Their inventory bulged at the seams, and the rumors of inferior quality in the bricks had proven untrue.

William continued to attend union meetings, asserting his influence in matters as much as he could.

With Hugh incarcerated, one vocal adversary had left the circle of dissenters, making things somewhat more relaxed.

To add to the change in attitudes, a new union president by the name of Osborne had taken office. Though no written prohibition of machine-made bricks existed, he influenced the council not to target businesses who pursued the manufacturing device. Unfortunately, a few rogue union members continued to do so on their own, and William had made sure that Cooper's property and yard were well guarded.

Taking a sip of tea, William thought about the day ahead. Christmas had passed, and Hugh would be released from prison that morning. He decided to be the one to greet him at the gate when it opened at nine o'clock. During the past year, the union and Hugh's comrades had all abandoned him during his imprisonment. Brown and Dodson had not kept their promise to watch out for Eliza nor had the union continued to support her household. Instead, she had been left to fend for herself and found work in a cotton mill while her neighbor, Phoebe, cared for the new baby and Margaret. Hugh had finally gotten the son he had wanted, and she named him Arthur. The lad was doing well, and William prayed that God would allow him to live a long life, unlike Thomas who died young.

William and Mary visited Eliza as often as he could, supplementing her income with ten shillings a week to help with food and other necessities. Above all, he wanted to keep her and the children out of the workhouse, which he knew Hugh feared would happen.

As the months passed, William never felt inclined to visit Hugh even though his imprisonment had been close to where he lived. Eliza rarely had the opportunity to see him. When she did, her description of the conditions and his physical appearance brought concern for his brother's welfare. New Bailey Prison was scheduled for closure because a new facility would open at Strangeways. Hugh would not have benefited since his release was beforehand.

William lifted his head as he heard Mary descend the staircase. Her right hand held her lower back, and her belly protruded to reveal her eighth month of pregnancy. When she placed her foot on the floor after the last step, she turned and waddled toward him. It was impossible not to beam at the sight of her. Regardless of her bulging womb and full breasts, she glowed in anticipation of motherhood.

"Stop snickering at me," she said, coming over and giving him a poke. "I feel like a fat duck."

"You look beautiful, quack… quack," he teased, grabbing her hand. She bent down and kissed him on the cheek.

"I swear, one more month, and this baby is coming out of me, and I shall scream bloody hell the entire time for what you've done to me, William Leighton."

"As long as everything goes well with you and the baby, you may scream as much as your heart desires. I shall be far away having a drink at the pub while the midwife brings our child into the world."

"You will not," she shot back at him. "You'll be right there in that chair, listening to the entire affair!"

William smiled mischievously. "You know I

wouldn't miss the event, my dear. I'm merely teasing you."

"Good." She plopped down on the chair, reached over, and took his hand. "How do you feel about today?"

"Apprehensive," he admitted, glancing at the clock on the mantel.

"Are you taking the day off at work?"

"Yes. Reggie, and I have discussed the matter at length." He fiddled with the rim of the teacup, tracing his finger along the edge. "It was no easy task to convince him of my scheme."

"Well, he did, and I think he continues to be a fair man, don't you agree?"

"Oh, absolutely," William concurred. "I owe him a tremendous amount for his faith in me and the opportunities to grow in the business."

"Does he still talk of a future partnership?" Mary's eyes lit up with a hopeful glint.

"Yes, as a matter of fact, he mentioned it only last week. Apparently the building of the new Manchester Town Hall is nearing the stage they'll be sending out bids to architects in December."

"I can't imagine the number of bricks needed for that job nor the cut stone for that matter. Surely the project will bring nothing but prosperity to workers and masters alike."

"You would think, but the union still frowns on machine-made bricks."

"Your power of persuasion shall turn the tide," Mary confidently remarked.

After glancing at his new pocket watch that actually kept time, he gulped the remaining tepid tea in his cup.

"I should be going," he announced, getting to his feet.

"Will you take him home first or bring him here?"

"Home, I should imagine. Eliza will be waiting with the children to greet him." William struggled with the uneasiness in his soul. He had no idea what to expect when he laid eyes on his brother. Hugh could accept his welcome or tell him to go to hell. The outcome weighed heavily upon his shoulders for he wanted nothing more than to heal the rift between them.

"I'm sure it will go fine," Mary said, embracing him and kissing him on the cheek. "Let's hope it's the prodigal son returning home."

"I hadn't thought of it that way, but I'm not sure if he's changed." William kissed her on the lips and let his hand rest upon her rounded belly, wondering if a boy or girl would be their gift.

He gave the driver directions to the destination with instructions to wait for another passenger. On the way, William struggled with a myriad of emotions, pondering their forthcoming reunion. Remnants of anger remained from the past, but William took control of his sentiments.

The crisp January morning gave way to a partly cloudy sky. William stood a few yards from the prison entrance. The sun early in the east hit the façade of the penitentiary, exposing its derelict condition. Anxious about the time, William pulled out his timekeeping device and observed the seconds tick by until he heard the rattle of iron and the hinges of the large door break the seal of security that held prisoners inside. William shoved his watch back in his pocket. His hands sweat from nerves as his eyes fixated on the opening. A group of three men exited, unsure of their steps and footing. Most of them put their hands above their brow to shield their eyes from the bright sun. Their disorientation at their surroundings obviously hindered their enthusiasm.

Williams's eyes fell upon the tallest in the group who appeared as a gangly form of skin and bones. Realizing that he gazed upon his brother, his breath hitched in shock at the stranger who emerged from the darkness of incarceration.

Hugh caught a glimpse of William and halted his step. The former gruff facial expression had disappeared into a shallow appearance of a man who gazed at him with hollow eyes. Unsure if he should approach, William waited for his brother to make the first move. After glancing around and noticing no one else, he shuffled forward like an old man. When he reached a yard away, he halted in front of William and without a smile or frown spoke one word.

"Brother."

Overcome by emotion at seeing him, William grabbed Hugh by the shoulder and pulled him forward, giving him a hearty pat on his back.

"Brothers indeed," he remarked with a shaky voice. Hugh made no movement to embrace him in return, and William detected the man he had once known had disappeared, leaving behind a broken shell.

He released him, and Hugh stared at him in return. After eyeing him up and down, he hesitantly spoke as if he could barely remember how to converse. "Appreciate you coming to get me."

"I've got a carriage, Hugh. Eliza is waiting for you at home."

"Me son still alive?" His brow rose with a hopeful look in his eye.

"Why yes, of course. He's a strapping young lad. Looks like you," William responded. Hugh hadn't barely the strength to climb into the carriage, and William gave him a hefty push to get him up the step and inside. Once the door closed and he settled back, his brother glanced around the interior in awe.

"Haven't seen anything this nice for quite a spell," he remarked. "Or anything that smelled that good either." Hugh lifted his gaze to William and studied him. "You're looking well. Things good? Work? Home?"

"Yes, good," William responded. "Mary is pregnant and due next month."

At last a small grin turned the corner of his mouth. "Well, I'll be damned. You're gonna be a father, eh?"

"By the look of her figure, it appears so."

Purposely he remained careful not to express too much about his situation, as it wasn't the right time. He watched his brother fall into silence, glancing out the window as if it were the first time he had seen the city. The hair on his head had thinned and grayed considerably. His complexion looked pale and shallow. William couldn't grasp how much weight he had lost, but after hearing of the poor diets prisoners were often given, it didn't surprise him. He thought about giving Eliza a few more shillings to stock up with some hearty meat dishes for Hugh's homecoming.

"They didn't take care of her, did they?" Hugh remarked, looking back with sadness in his eyes.

"You mean the union?"

"Yeah."

William shook his head no. "For a short time but then nothing."

"I suppose I should thank you for keeping 'em out of the workhouse," Hugh remarked. "Done worried about 'em the whole time I was gone."

"I'm an uncle to Arthur and Margaret," William remarked. "Of course I helped."

"How's Eliza? Haven't seen her much. Her crying when she visited done me no good. Told her not to come back."

"She's fine, Hugh. In spite of her tears, she's a surprisingly strong woman."

The carriage slowed as they approached Hugh's residence. Perhaps William should have moved them to a better place, but Eliza insisted she wanted to stay until Hugh returned. He looked anxiously out the window and sucked in a shaky breath when they came to a halt in front of his home. William exited first to help Hugh, but he refused.

"I can do it meself," he replied. "Not crippled yet." As soon as his foot hit the street, the door to his residence flew open and Eliza came running out to greet him. Hugh remained rigid in the place his feet had landed. When his wife flung her arms around him, he lost his balance.

"Hold on, woman," he said. "You're gonna knock me over."

"Oh, Hugh, I've missed you so," she gushed,

kissing him repeatedly.

William watched the exchange, but Hugh acted too tired to muster up an ounce of emotion to give his wife in return. Of course, when he had left a year ago, their relationship had been anything but close.

"So you done gave me a son, did you?" he asked, eyeing her empty belly.

"Aye. Do you want to see him?"

"Sure do," he said, walking toward the door. Hugh halted and glanced at William. "Don't mind if I am alone now, do you?"

"No, don't mind, Hugh. We can talk another time."

Expecting to depart anyway and leave Hugh to his reunion, William climbed back in the carriage. When his brother settled into life again, he would let him know that a job would be waiting for him back at Cooper's if he wanted it.

Chapter Twenty~Seven

A PARTNERSHIP BEGINS

A month passed since Hugh's return to Eliza and his children. William gave him the opportunity to acclimate back into daily life. When he felt ready to return to work, he made him the offer to come and work for Cooper. The opportunity had put a slight strain on William's relationship with his employer because at first he refused to allow Hugh to work at the company. After what he had done, William knew Hugh would never find work again in Manchester. The painful reality became apparent to Hugh as well.

Convinced that the union's failure to support him through the ordeal of imprisonment left a bitter taste in his brother's mouth, he no longer had any desire to participate in the council or its enforcement activities that might lead him back to the hell he had lived in during the past twelve months.

Reggie agreed to let him work in the clay fields at first. If Hugh proved himself worthy, they decided to allow him to return to bricklaying. Their business had grown from making bricks to that of general contracting and had started to build a team of experienced bricklayers on their workforce. Also, they were subcontracting out to masons for stonework and joiners for carpentry.

Hugh, grateful for the job, accepted it with a slight hesitation and reported for his first day of work.

"This means you're me foreman?" he grumbled. "Not sure I can take getting orders from me younger brother."

"Mr. Cooper is training me to do other things," William replied. "Won't be much of a foreman cracking the whip at you out in the field."

Hugh's face turned sour. "Never thought I'd be back slinging clay."

"Won't be for long, Hugh. Keep your nose clean, and Mr. Cooper will have you laying bricks soon. He just needs to put his trust in you, that's all."

"Trust," Hugh repeated. "Never put much stock in the word until now. Best I learn how to earn it."

"Best you do," William replied.

As they were talking, William caught sight of Reggie running in his direction from the office with a panicked expression on his face.

"William!" He drew near and slapped his hand on his shoulder. "Come quick, man, your wife's having a baby."

"Now?" he screeched.

"Now, man, get going. The midwife is at your house along with Miss Beecham."

"Go," Hugh said, giving him a slight push. "It's about time you became a father."

He grinned at William, and it was the first time he had seen his brother express any amusement since his release from prison. The experience inside had never been mentioned in conversation, and William figured that if Hugh wanted to bring it up, he would.

All he knew at that moment was that his brother had returned, apparently a better person for what he suffered, and that was good enough for him.

Each step William ran felt as if it took an eternity to reach his home. When he arrived, he burst through the door and stood in the middle of the room, expecting to hear Mary's screams coming from upstairs. Instead, there was silence, and it frightened him. He ran up only to be halted by Miss Beecham. Her hand was in the air as if she were directing carriages on a Manchester street in town center. Her face showed no emotion, and for a split second, William thought the worst had happened. Miriam shook her head back and forth and finally spoke.

"Never in my entire life have I witnessed one woman push out a baby so fast as your wife," she said with a smile upturning her lips. "I'm afraid, Mr. Leighton, you should brace yourself for a large brood of children if this is how easy she births them."

"It's over already?" he asked, astonished at Miriam's remark.

"Yes, and you have a darling baby daughter."

"Can I see her?" His voice quavered.

"Sure, mother and daughter are resting."

Miriam opened the door and peeked inside. The midwife was cleaning up the bedding, and she looked around the edge of the door. "Is it safe for the father to come in?"

"Of course," she said.

William didn't wait for further invitation. He pushed open the door with his left hand to reveal Mary holding a baby in her arms.

"Look, William, we have a daughter." Mary's face,

in spite of having just given birth, beamed with joy.

Slowly he approached, astonished at how small the baby cradled in his wife's arms appeared. "She's so tiny," he remarked, gazing down at her in awe. Mary turned her little face in his direction, revealing the cutest thing he had ever laid eyes on.

"You're not sorry it isn't a boy, are you?" Mary looked up at him with slight apprehension.

"The way you give birth," Miriam remarked, "there will be plenty of other opportunities for boys."

"No, of course, not," he said.

"Do you want to hold her?"

Not sure he was ready, he stepped back. "Don't know about holding babies."

"Oh, William, don't be so afraid. Come here. I'll show you how."

He figured he better get on with it, so he neared Mary as she held out his daughter.

"Put one hand under her head. Babies have weak necks when they are born. Put the other under her and just cradle her in your arms. It will be all right."

A tremble of excitement shook his hands as he held the newborn.

"See, you're doing just fine, isn't he, Miriam?"

"Yes, he'll get the hang of it."

William gazed down at his daughter, filled with awe at the gift of life, and gulped at the overwhelming responsibility of fatherhood.

"I want at least five or six more children," Mary announced.

William's eyes widened at her comment. "We haven't even named the first one." He balked. "Getting ahead of yourself, aren't you?"

"Have you thought of a name yet," Miriam inquired.

"You know Mary, always prepared. She already had her mind made up, and though I think it's a bit regal in nature, I agreed."

"Well, what is it?"

"Gwendolyn," Mary replied.

"Oh, my, it is a bit regal, isn't it?" Miriam scoffed. "Lady Gwendolyn."

"Don't think so now," William replied. "She looks like a princess to me."

The baby suddenly started to wail, scaring the daylights out of him. "Now what?"

"Give her back," Mary said, holding out her arms.

"The baby needs feeding," the midwife announced. "And your wife needs rest. Best you go now, Mr. Leighton, and let the little one get nourishment." She shooed him away with her hand.

Mary didn't appear overwhelmed after giving birth, but she glanced at him, giving a reassuring nod that she was all right.

"Call me if you need me," he said.

"Okay, time to go." Miriam pointed toward the door.

William obeyed and wandered downstairs in a daze. His hands still trembled from the news and experience. He could use a drink but hadn't kept a drop of alcohol in the household. As he sat down to relax for a moment, a knock came at the door. He opened it to see Reggie standing on the stoop with a bottle of whiskey and a box of cigars.

"You a father yet?" he asked, holding up the gifts in hand.

"You bet I am. Fine young baby girl."

"You rascal, you," Reggie said. "Congratulations and welcome to parenthood."

"Come on in." William stepped aside. "I just wished for a stiff drink."

"Well, a gulp of Irish whiskey will do the trick," he announced, setting the bottle down on the table. "Got two glasses?"

William retrieved two and watched Reggie open the bottle and pour an inch in each one.

"Here you go," he said. "A toast to you and your family and your fine young lass. May she grow up to be the joy of your soul and have a good life filled with blessings."

Overwhelmed, his eyes teared at the thought. "Thanks, Reggie," he replied. "You've been a good employer and also a friend."

They tapped glasses and took a drink together. Reggie opened the box of cigars. "I suppose we should have a smoke outdoors later. If your wife is anything like mine, smoking in the house isn't much appreciated when it comes to cigars."

"I suppose not," William said.

"So listen, William," Reggie began, sitting confidently back in the chair. "I've been waiting for this day."

"As I," William replied, cocking his head, a bit confused at the remark.

"I have something I want to show you." Reggie reached inside his vest pocket and pulled out a calling card. "Had these printed in anticipation of today." He handed it to William, who took it in hand.

William regarded the print and frowned, not

understanding what he was reading. The card had the names of COOPER & LEIGHTON in a fine script written across the center, and underneath the words BRICKMAKERS, BRICKLAYERS, AND CONTRACTORS, HIGHER BROUGHTON.

"I don't… I don't understand," William sputtered, staring at the card.

"What's there to understand?" Reggie put his hand on William's shoulder. "I'm making you my partner, William. I can't grow this business any further by myself. Need you at my side to take it to the next level."

"But I—"

"There are times I believe in you more than you believe in yourself," Reggie stated. "That's why I'm not asking you, I'm telling you. Printed the cards and have thousands on hand. Too late to back out now, partner." He held out his hand toward William. "Just need you to shake hands and sign some papers. Take the week off and be with your wife. When you come back, it will be Cooper & Leighton."

Unsure how to process the overwhelming gift of partnership, William didn't wish to offend Reggie a moment longer. He reached out his hand and grabbed it tightly, giving it a hearty shake in return. "You've got a partner," he said, grinning from ear to ear.

"Good choice, Leighton. By the time we're done, our business will be the talk of the town."

"Your generosity is overwhelming, Reggie."

"It's a selfish move on my part, actually. It takes a man to realize you can't do everything on your own. You need good people around you to succeed. Men with ambition and integrity like yourself. I wouldn't trust my business to any other person but you."

William gulped the whiskey in his glass and then held it out. "I think I could use another."

Reggie nodded his head. "I could use one too."

It had been a day of gifts—fatherhood and partnership. Mary would be ecstatic about the news that no longer would he be the slave.

Epilogue

SLAVE TO NONE

In March 1867, the town clerk for Manchester issued a set of specifications for architects on the new town hall. The first of July had been the deadline for designers to submit their proposals. The building, located at Albert Square, Princess Street, and Cooper Street, would be an ambitious endeavor. The town hall would have a basement, ground floor, grand main entrance, and four stories of rooms that consisted of meeting halls, reception rooms, private quarters, council chambers, and the like.

Reggie and William paid attention to the timeline, waiting for the final selection of the architect and for upcoming bids for bricks. Their business stood ready and able to meet demand, along with other brickmakers in the Manchester district who had the apparatuses. As a result, the union received additional pressure to release its objection to machine-made bricks.

In the meantime, Reggie and William settled into a routine of partnership. Reggie hired a clerk for the office to help with the books, a new foreman to replace William, and had increased staff as new projects were awarded.

It hadn't been easy for Hugh to settle back into

work at the bottom of the chain of command. Reggie agreed that he needn't stay long in the fields. William brought him out and placed him on bricklaying jobs, increasing his pay to get him out of the slum neighborhood where he lived. He rented a terrace house off Fenney Street as well, which had become a popular place for many of the workers at their business to reside.

The gentry landowners eventually allowed more development in the area but still kept a tight hand on Higher Broughton's growth. Reggie wanted to purchase the brickfields and started price negotiations. If they could convince owners to sell off parcels of their land, the investment would only increase their personal net worth.

The relationship between Hugh and William started to repair though some fundamental differences remained between the two. Hugh hadn't found religion to be much help, and some of his liberal ideas that bordered on socialism still rumbled underneath. Finally, when he could find the strength to speak of it, he chatted openly about his year in prison.

"There's only one purpose behind 'em walls," he said with a grim look in his eye. "It's breaking the spirit of the men inside. They make it hell so you don't wanna come back again."

William wanted to say he was sorry that he had to endure it, but the fact remained, he had put himself there by his actions.

"I still wake up with nightmares," he confessed. "Eliza don't know how to deal with it. Get down in spirits sometimes too. Angry at the world—angry at meself."

"I suppose it will take some time to recover," William replied. "You're alive, and that's all that matters to me. I was worried you might not make it out," William confessed.

"At times I wished I would die so it would end. Bad enough I killed a horse, but some buggers in there did far worse than me. Of course, the murderers get hung right away, so that leaves you with the thieves, fraudsters, rapists, thugs, and other trash."

William didn't know how to respond, so he listened as Hugh talked about the lack of food, beatings by the guards, hard labor, and every other horror imaginable. When he ended, he gazed at Hugh with empathy.

"You did good for yourself, William. Partner now with Cooper. How'd you manage that?"

William smirked. "Got to ask you a question first," he said. "The warehouse I was working at, did you participate in the destruction of the bricks that night?"

"You pretty much figured out already that I did. Why'd you ask?"

"Well, if I hadn't lost my job, I would have never met Mr. Cooper. I was in a pub, having an ale to drown my sorrows when he approached, asking questions about the union. Told me he wanted to start a business and gave me his card."

"Is that right?" His eyes brightened at the revelation.

"So you see," William began, "you had your hand in pushing me toward good fortune and a stroke of luck."

"I'll be damned." Hugh laughed. "Done did you right then after all your complaining."

"Guess you did."

They both glanced at one another, and for the first time in years, William felt the comradery of brothers return. By the glint in Hugh's eyes, he felt the same.

"So, who's going to have the next child—Eliza or Mary?" William asked with a snicker.

"Oh, I'm already working on it," Hugh said, laughing aloud.

"Boy or girl?"

"Another boy. Going to breed me own young strapping bricklayers to take me place when I leave this earth." He smiled at William. "And you?"

"Oh, I don't know. Partial to girls, I guess, but I'll take my chance with a few young lads as well."

"How 'bout we go get a drink and toast to our future generation," Hugh said.

"Sounds good to me," William remarked.

The two left together, joking on the way to the pub. Hugh slung his arm around William's shoulder, and with each step they took, the broken relationship mended.

The Leighton Family Saga

To read more about the research behind The Leighton Family Saga, visit and follow the blog at the <u>https://leighton-saga-books.com.</u>

Book One—Toil Under the Sun
Book Two—Slave to None
Book Three—Just for All
Book Four—Vanishing Vapor

About the Author

With Russian blood on my father's side and English on my mother's, I blame my ancestors for the lethal combination of my DNA that influences my stories. Tragedy and drama might be found between the pages, but I eventually give readers a happy ending.

I live in the scenic but rainy Pacific Northwest. My hobby (more of an obsession) is researching my English ancestry and expanding my family tree. To keep the memory of my ancestors alive, I often use their names in my novels.

My usual genre is historical fiction with romantic elements and historical romance set in the Victorian and Edwardian eras. My books include:

The Price of Innocence (Permanently Free)—Book One of the Legacy Series

The Price of Deception—Book Two of the Legacy Series

The Price of Love—Book Three of the Legacy Series

The Price of Passion—Book Four of the Legacy Series

The Legacy Series Box Set (Books 1–4)

The Phantom of Valletta (Featured in the *Sunday*

Times, Malta in 2010)

Dark Persuasion (2012 Finalist in the USA Best Book Awards for Romance)

A Portrait of Perfection (A Dark Gothic Tale of Love and Betrayal)

A Christmas Oath (2015 Christmas Novelette)

A Christmas Mission (2016 Christmas Novelette)

Lady Isabella (2017)

Lady Grace (2017)

Lady Charlotte (2018)

Romance with a Kiss of Suspense, under the pen name of Nora Covington. Works to date include:

Thorncroft Manor

Whitefield Hall

Blythe Court—Five-Star Readers' Favorite Review

Romance with a Kiss of Suspense Box Set

Conflicting Hearts, by J. D. Burrows, contemporary romance/women's fiction. Winning Finalist in 2017 Reader's Favorite Book Awards for Fiction: Social Issues.

You can find me on: https://vickihopkins.com

The best way to thank an author is to write a review. Thank you.